create your
erotic
fantasy

kathryn in the city

mary anne mohanraj

MELCHER
MEDIA

GOTHAM BOOKS

For David and for Heather;
for some paths taken and others not
—MARY ANNE MOHANRAJ

GOTHAM BOOKS
Published by Penguin Group (USA) Inc.
375 Hudson Street, New York, New York 10014, U.S.A.
Penguin Books Ltd., 80 Strand, London WC2R 0RL, England
Penguin Books Australia Ltd., 250 Camberwell Road, Camberwell, Victoria 3124, Australia
Penguin Books Canada Ltd., 10 Alcorn Avenue, Toronto, Ontario M4V 3B2, Canada
Penguin Books (N.Z.) Ltd., Cnr Rosedale and Airborne Roads, Albany, Auckland 1310, New Zealand

Penguin Books Ltd., Registered Offices: 80 Strand, London WC2R 0RL, England
Published by Gotham Books, a division of Penguin Group (USA) Inc.

First printing, June 2003
1 3 5 7 9 10 8 6 4 2

LIBRARY OF CONGRESS CATALOGING-IN-PUBLICATION DATA
is available.

Printed in the United States of America
Set in Garamond and Bodoni Book

PUBLISHER'S NOTE

a note to readers

This is not like other books. The individuals you encounter, the places you go, and the sexual risks you take are all entirely up to you. There is only one certainty: if you read this book over and over, you will have a wildly different, erotically charged experience each time.

As you make your way through the book, you will be presented with a series of choices at key moments. With each new decision made, you will be directed to a different page. Ever dream of trying a threesome? A foursome? How about auditioning at a strip club? Or engaging in more than a little S&M? What you do next is entirely in your hands. If things don't turn out the way you imagined, simply turn back to the beginning and start all over again.

The choice—and the fantasy—is all yours.

It's raining in San Francisco when you arrive, a cool drizzle that soaks through your thin sweater and chills your skin. Everything looks gray and dingy. It was warm on the bus, and warmer back home, in Greendale, Indiana. You left on a beautiful April day, with the sun high and not a cloud in the sky—a perfect day for a wedding. It would have been your wedding day.

You're standing in front of a locked gate, searching for the right name: Reyes. Rose Reyes, a friend of your best girlfriend, Sally. Sally took off last year, just dropped out of college and started traveling the world. Her letters had made you itchy, her stories of adventure and excitement. Mostly sexual adventure—crossing the ocean had turned your friend into what you normally would have called a total slut. Sally loved shocking you with stories about picking up strange men in cafés and bus stops; she'd gotten off on crowded trains, rented rooms by the hour in London and Tokyo—and ended up staying in those rooms for days on end. Sometimes there were handcuffs involved. You had to burn the letters after you read them, in case your mother found them. The way Sally talked about sex, about the feel of hands on her body, a man's mouth on her skin—it sounded amazing, like fireworks. John had been more like a box of damp matches. You could strike a spark eventually, but it took hours.

You're not supposed to be thinking about John. You're not engaged anymore, no longer the perfect fiancée, just out of college and ready to be wed. You left all of that behind in Greendale, along with poor, bewildered John. You're single, you're sexy, you're ready for adventure. That's what you keep telling yourself.

There's that name on the buzzer, Reyes. Oddly, there's another name along with it, O'Reilly. O'Reilly? Sally hadn't mentioned another roommate. You hope she's nice. You hope they both are. Enough stalling—you take a deep breath and push the buzzer. Even though it's stopped raining, your sweater is still almost soaked through. You're shivering.

"Kathryn? Is that you?" The voice is crackly with static but clearly female.

"Yes—Rose?"

"That's me! C'mon up—fifth floor!"

The buzzer unlocks the gate, and you push it open.

• PLEASE TURN TO PAGE 68.

Y ou just hadn't been thinking. Something about Michael makes it very hard to think. But in the few minutes he's gone, you think pretty hard—about sex with your roommate, with your roommate who has a boyfriend, about what a dumb idea that would be.

When Michael slips back in and closes the door, a foil packet in his hand and a thick cock jutting out in front, he finds you dressed again, flannel firmly back on and your arms wrapped tightly around your knees.

"We can't do this, Michael. You make me crazy, but this is not a good idea. I'm so sorry." Your voice is firm—it's the same voice you used to tell John you were leaving him. You're getting good at calling things off.

Michael takes a few steps forward, until he's barely an inch away. He reaches out and tilts your chin up. "Well, I can't say I'm not disappointed, sweet Kate. You taste delicious, and I was looking forward to exploring you further." His eyes are locked on yours, and his words are making your pussy cream. But your arms stay tight right where they are. You've made your decision, and you're sure it's the right one. Pretty sure. He shrugs and releases your chin. "I guess I'll just have to enjoy my memories."

"Sorry." You want to look down, but that seems cowardly. You keep your eyes on his. "Can we be friends?"

He take a deep breath, manages a smile. "No worries. I'm going to go find a nice friendly shower now, though. I'll see you in a bit. We'll talk about that computer job." He turns and walks to the door.

"Thanks, Michael. Thanks for everything."

He turns and grins. "My pleasure. Really." He opens the door and walks out, closing it softly behind him. You lie back on the bed, pulling a blanket up over you, thinking about what you turned down. It's a while before you manage to get up again.

When you do come out into the kitchen, it's to see Michael at the kitchen table, eating breakfast, looking perfectly calm, as if nothing has happened. Your stomach twists a little, but you're determined to shake it off. You walk into the kitchen and say good morning, as if this is the first you've seen of him today. Michael has the right idea—it's best to pretend that nothing happened in your bedroom. You're not sure how easy pretending will be. You get yourself another cup of coffee, lean on the counter, and take deep breaths, trying not to look too hard at Michael.

• PLEASE TURN TO PAGE 58.

You're sitting alone in a room, on a raised platform. Two walls of glass—one facing the hallway, one facing another small room, both with curtains that you can pull. You leave the hallway one open for now and sit, leaning back on some cushions there, trying to look enticing. The gown's lying by your side; you're just in red bra and panties, black garters, stockings and heels. You smile at the men who walk by, who pause and look at you. Trying to get them to open the door, to turn the knob, to come in. To negotiate for your services—whatever services you can perform through glass, over a microphone. This is a very strange thing. And it's only your second day in San Francisco. Is this what you wanted from the big city?

A man pauses outside your window. You slide your legs open, just a little. Not enough for him to see much of anything. But the motion, the invitation, is apparently enough. He's opening the door. He's coming in. He's closing the door behind him, and you're opening his curtain and closing the one to the outside world. Now it's the two of you in a tight space divided by glass. The glass is a good thing.

He's opening his coat, sliding a handful of tissues into the waistband of his sweatpants. His eyes are on you, on your breasts.

"Take off your bra. I want to see your breasts."

"Twenty bucks." You have no idea if that's a reasonable amount. He doesn't seem to care, though, simply fumbles out a wallet with his other hand and stuffs a twenty into the slot. Easy money.

For that, you figure you'll give him a show, at least. You shift to your knees, facing him. You start taking off your bra, slowly. You rub your breasts through the lace, pinch the hard nipples. You slide the straps down.

"Just take it off." His hand is moving in his pants.

Well, he paid for it. You reach behind and unhook the strap, drop the bra. Now your breasts are there, naked, hanging full and heavy. His tongue slips out, and his hand moves faster. You're not sure what to do. He doesn't seem to want you to do anything, only sit there, a bare-breasted icon.

He starts muttering softly, almost inaudibly. "Fuck. Yes. Fuck, yes, you bitch. Gorgeous bitch. Gorgeous fucking breasts, fucking cunt." He's pumping faster, harder, and a thin line of drool slides out the corner of his mouth. "Huge goddamned fucking breasts, you cunt. You stupid gorgeous cunt." He's tilting his head back, but his eyes are still fixed on your breasts, your thick pink nipples.

Do you have to take this? Is this what it's supposed to be like? Shouldn't you get paid extra?

"Hey—it'll be another twenty dollars if you want to say that stuff."

"Fucking bitch!" He comes then, in a gasp and a jerk. Before you can say anything, he's putting two more twenties through the slot, nodding his thanks, and disappearing out the door, a wad of soiled tissues clutched in his hand.

- *If you want to stay in the booth,* PLEASE TURN TO PAGE 107.

- *If you want to go back to the apartment and try a computer job instead,* PLEASE TURN TO PAGE 94.

- *If the whole experience makes you feel queasy—if you just want to go home, really home,* PLEASE TURN TO PAGE 135.

Rose is a slender girl with light brown skin and tilted almond eyes; she looks like some kind of ethnic mix. Her hair is a wonderful wet mane, streaked with blond and brown and even a little red. But what's surprising is that she's wearing only a skimpy white bra and white panties—doesn't anyone wear clothes in this city?

"You know, you've got to put clothes *on* if you want to take them off, Rosie." Mike grins as he helps himself to a cup of hot chocolate from the tray.

"Hot chocolate, Kathryn? I'm sorry to be so crazy today, but one of the other girls called in sick, so they need me to come in a few hours early. I'm not sure if Sally mentioned that I work as a stripper?" Rose turns a little and bends, setting the tray on a low crate that seems to be serving as an end table. The panties are thongs. You can't help staring at Rose's ass. Two perfectly shaped buttocks— you'd kill for an ass like that. You've always thought yours was too skinny. No wonder Rose is a stripper.

"No—no, Sally didn't mention that." You keep your voice calm, friendly. You're cool. You can handle this. Your roommate is a stripper!

"Jamie's still at work, but he'll be home soon," Michael says. "He's an accountant, very good with the rent. You'll love him."

"Him?" Not just one man here—two? Is Jamie Rose's boyfriend, then? Or maybe *Mike* is Rose's boyfriend? They'd certainly look good together, all browns and golds.

Rose frowns a little. "Sally didn't tell you my roommates were a couple? Mike and Jamie have been together just forever. They're very stable roommates."

"No, no, she didn't." Sally hadn't mentioned much of anything, it seems. You're going to kill her. Honestly, you're having a hard time taking it all in. Rose is a stripper who wanders around the apartment half dressed in front of a relative stranger, *and* she has two gay roommates? Does that cover everything? Are you really ready to handle San Francisco? You'd known that the city was full of gay people, but to actually be living with some. . . . They'd be having gay sex in the next bedroom. You don't even know what two men *do* together. Your mother would have a heart attack if she heard. Part of you wants to get right back on the bus and head straight home to Greendale.

Or you could try to be a grown-up about it; your roommates might be half dressed, and two of them might be gay, but it's not as if any of them are trying to seduce you. You could reach out and take a cup of hot chocolate. What could be more harmless and domestic than hot chocolate?

• *If you decide to stick it out a little longer,* PLEASE TURN TO PAGE 181.

• *If you decide to turn around and go back to Indiana,* PLEASE TURN TO PAGE 187.

You take a deep breath, close your eyes, and open them again. "I'll try it."

Rose grins. "Hey, good for you! I know, it's all kind of scary at first. But trust me, you get used to it quickly. C'mon—I'll introduce you to the girls."

She leads you out of the little room, down the hall, past a large Plexiglas window where a blond girl sits cross-legged, smiling. "That's the private show—it's where you make the real money. If they like you, you'll get to try it later." Down a flight of stairs to a large room, brightly lit, full of half-dressed women. She introduces you to a flurry of women with names you can't remember and that aren't theirs in any case. There are others Rose doesn't know—more amateurs, trying out. The competition. You check them out surreptitiously as you undress: they all look normal, not particularly stunning. Just normal women, kind of pretty, kind of sexy. They don't *look* like fallen women. Your mother would be shocked.

You're trying not to think too much about what you're doing—pulling off your T-shirt and jeans, slipping out of your plain cotton underwear. It's just like being in the women's locker room at the gym, though you always changed in a cubicle, not out in the open. In Indiana, you'd been modest, even a little shy. But that was Kathryn—nice Kathryn, good Kathryn, her mother's favorite daughter. John's proper little fiancée. Now you aren't Kathryn anymore—you're Angela. And Angela will be a shameless slut, if she wants to be. You pull on the red lace panties, the red bra. The thigh-high stockings that clip into a garter belt in a complicated fashion that Rose has to demonstrate. The stiletto heels. And over the whole thing, the flowing black gown.

You look at yourself in the mirror—it's a good look. Elegant, classy. It would be even better with elbow-length black gloves. And if you grew your hair out again, you could put it up at the beginning of the act, then pull it down again. But for now, short and wavy around your shoulders will have to do. You like the way it feels, at least, brushing your shoulders. Sensual, soft. You brush a little lipstick on, dark red. It's Rose's—a color you never would have worn at home.

Rose looks you up and down approvingly. She's skimmed into her own outfit while you dressed and thrown a robe over it. "You look great, Angela. Fabulous. You ready?"

You bite your lip, nodding.

"Terrific. It's showtime."

There's a mass of you waiting by the door to the stage—so many girls trying out tonight. The door opens and you go in. It's hard to see at first; the room is barely lit with dim reddish light. There are glass windows everywhere, some of them opening already to reveal the tiny dark rooms where men are waiting. You can't focus on that yet, though—you're trying to find a place not too far out in front, where you can catch your breath, listen to the music, maybe start to dance.

A redhead in front of you is throwing herself into it already, hips gyrating, bending forward and holding her huge naked breasts in her hands. Her big ass is practically in your face. You can't do that, not quite yet. You can't even look at the other girls, much less the men. You close your eyes. You're not you—you're Angela. Angela can do this.

Angela starts swaying to the music, something slow and sexy that you can't place but you're almost certain you've heard before. Her hands slide up and down the gown, caressing her thighs, her hips, her waist. Angela has done this a hundred times—maybe not here but for lovers. She has many lovers, and they all like to watch her dance for them. This is a private dance for one of them, a ruggedly handsome man, a powerful, rich man who could have any girl he wants but has chosen her. He watches her cup her breasts. He's whispering to her, urging her to take off the gown, please. Please, Angela, take that off. He needs to see her naked.

She bends forward, giving him a glimpse of breasts; she reaches down and gathers two handfuls of gown in her hands. She pulls it up slowly, so slowly. They've got all night; they have a hundred, a thousand, nights ahead of them. She shows him slender calves in black stockings, long, lean thighs striped with garter straps. The gown slides farther up, revealing the red panties, the black garter belt, a smooth stomach. Angela pauses there, rocking her hips, feeling his eyes on her. She can do this—she likes doing this. She opens her eyes then and catches the gaze of the man in the booth across from her. The window starts to close and then opens again—he's put another quarter in; his eyes are fixed on her and he can't bear to miss anything. He adores her. Angela smiles at him, though she can barely make out his face, pressed to the glass. She pulls the gown up above her head, exposing her red bra and the breasts almost spilling out of it. She drops the gown next to her and smiles. The man is still riveted. Angela's liking this. She's doing well.

Another girl leans over and whispers to her, "Slow down—you're half undressed and we've got time to kill in here. You're going to have to stick things in yourself if you keep up that pace."

Maybe Angela isn't doing as well as she thought.

• PLEASE TURN TO PAGE 131.

Y ou reach out and take Michael's other hand, bringing them both together until they're enclosed in yours—as much as they can be, given the largeness of them and the smallness of yours.

"Listen, Michael—I like you."

"I like you, too, Katie-girl."

"That's good. That's really good. Because the thing is . . ."

"Yes?"

"The thing is, I don't want to share you. I'm not a sharing sort of person. What I want is to date you, just you. We can explore this relationship, see where things are going."

"Katie—Kathryn, look, I like you. But I don't like you enough to break up with Jamie for you."

"But I thought the sex—"

"The sex was great, don't get me wrong. But it was just sex. You've had sex before, haven't you?"

"Not like that."

"Well, I'm sorry, then. But you're going to have to trust me, it was just great sex. It doesn't mean that we're soul mates, it doesn't mean that we have some higher spiritual connection—it didn't mean anything. Only that I liked you and thought you were hot."

"Oh. So, where does that leave us?"

"Well, that's up to you, isn't it? The offer's still open, if you want to have lunch with Jamie. Or we can call this whole thing off and stick to being good roommates, and hopefully friends. Oh, by the way, I set up a tentative job interview for you at my company at three today, if you want it. Either one's OK with me, sweetheart. It's up to you."

You can't believe that it was just sex for him: it felt like so much more to you. You really don't want to talk to Jamie; you know now that you're not a sharing kind of girl. Maybe you should call the whole thing off. Or maybe, just maybe, you should make a bold move. What would Sally do in this situation? Would she walk away from a hot guy like this? Or would she dive in, grab hold, and take what she wanted? What kind of woman are you, anyway?

• *If you decide to give up on Michael*, PLEASE TURN TO PAGE 165.

• *If you choose to get more aggressive*, PLEASE TURN TO PAGE 143.

Y ou knock hesitantly and peek in.

"Hey, roomie!" A man greets you, a stunningly handsome man. He's wearing only a pair of bike shorts, which means that you can't help but get a good look at his sculpted body, broad and taut, with particularly muscled thighs—he must bike a lot. On San Francisco's hills, that's hard work. A dark tan, too—it must be sunny here sometimes. Straight white-blond hair that falls across his face, sharp blue eyes. What Sally would have called a heartbreaker in one of her letters. Right before she went for him. The idea of a male roommate is a little strange, but maybe . . .

"I'm Mike, Michael O'Reilly. And you'll be Kathryn."

"That's right." You put down your duffel bag and shake hands. Nice big hands; you've always liked strong hands in a man. A few minutes ago you were thinking about Peter's hands, now you're fascinated by Mike's. You wonder what his hands would feel like against your skin. They look solid and warm; you're so cold, but a few minutes with those hands on you and you'd warm right up. Better yet, his whole body pressed against yours, pressing you against a wall— that'd be really warm. With thighs like that, he could probably hold you up for hours without breaking a sweat, though it'd be better if he did break a sweat. He'd look really good with sweat beading on those smooth planes of muscle, that tanned skin. But you can't keep thinking this way, jeez. First the cute professor in the stairwell, now this one. You don't know this guy at all. He probably has a girlfriend. A guy this gorgeous has to have a girlfriend.

He smiles as he lets go of your hand. "Oh, and here's Rose with the hot chocolate. It gets chilly in this city; we drink a lot of hot drinks. You like hot chocolate?"

You turn to see the mysterious Rose—you'd gotten only a brief description of her in Sally's letters. You're startled by what you see grinning at you. "Sorry," she says as she walks down the hall, "I would have thrown on more clothes, but I'm in a huge rush. Gotta finish drying my hair and get to work."

• PLEASE TURN TO PAGE 7.

It's a strange job, what you're doing here. You had thought it might be fun, but you hadn't expected it to be so sexy, to push you into doing things you'd read about in romance novels but never thought you'd do yourself. Because good girls don't. Because Kathryn used to be a good girl. It'd be easy to put it all on Angela, the persona, but you know better. You know that the things you've liked doing here, that was all you. That was Kathryn. This job is more than a job—it's a way to learn who you are, what you want, what you really like. It's a way to push yourself, push your own boundaries, go further than you've ever gone before. You can do this. You can be a peep-show girl. You can like it, and like it a lot.

Not to mention that you'll have made at least twice as much in half an hour here, even after the house takes its cut, than you ever have before. Even with an occasional creep, this could be a pretty good gig, here in San Francisco. Anything else could happen—you might meet a nice guy (or girl), you might fall in love. But for now you have cool roommates, a job that'll pay the rent with quite a bit left over, and probably at least a few screaming orgasms a night.

If this is life in the big city, it's not half bad.

THE END

You tilt your head back a little, enough to let Michael know that you're liking this. Your fingers spread against his bare chest, and your legs in their damp jeans press forward against his. He kisses you a little harder, and his hand starts wandering up and down your body, still over your clothes. It's strange—you haven't kissed anyone except your ex-fiancé in over two years. Strange but nice, very nice. The tingle has definitely spread below your collarbone, reaching your breasts, still encased in a bra and the thin cotton tank, pressing tightly against the backs of your hands.

Michael bites gently at your lower lip, and your fingers clench against him. His hand slips underneath your tank top, fingers tracing patterns up and down your spine, almost as if he's spelling out words. You can't concentrate enough to make them out, if so; his lips still moving against yours make it impossible to think. You open your mouth and your tongue slips out, wet against his lips. Michael opens his mouth, too, sucks your tongue lightly against his teeth while his hand is pushing your tank up, baring your black cotton bra. Your nipples are hard against his hands, clearly outlined through the fabric. His mouth leaves yours, and you moan softly at the betrayal, but then his lips are kissing your chin, your neck, your collarbone. Tracing a path slowly and surely down to where your nipples are now aching for him, he slides right past your breasts and kisses your stomach, dipping his tongue into your navel until you can't help squirming. He slides down farther—it's a big bed. Plenty of room for this. His mouth is nipping at the flesh right above the button on your jeans, but he doesn't move on. You're tingling all over and it's driving you crazy, but he keeps on, licking and sucking the skin, until you figure out that he's waiting for you to make the next move.

You don't want to think about it. You reach down, unbutton your jeans, and zip the fly down, baring a triangle of black cotton panties. He takes over then, his hands on your hips, pulling down the jeans. You lift your ass to make it easier for him. It still takes a long time—the jeans are wet, and tight enough that he has to peel them off you. He goes slow, kissing the hollow of your hip, your thighs, your knees as he goes. You keep your eyes closed—if you don't see what he's doing, you don't have to think about it much. You're too busy concentrating on the sensations anyway—the feather brushes along your shaking legs, the wet lines he traces with his tongue.

➤

Finally the jeans are off, and he slides back up, just far enough that his mouth is hovering over the juncture of your thighs. Your legs are still closed; Michael puts his hands on them and moves them apart, firmly. You don't resist— you don't want to. Instead, you reach down and curl your fingers through his soft hair. He's resting between your outstretched legs, breathing against your cotton-clad pussy, hot breath that sends shivers running through your entire body. He licks you through the cotton—it feels incredible, but so strange. John never put his mouth down there. He thought it was dirty; he didn't let you put your mouth on his penis, either. You'd suggested his going down there only once, though you'd thought about it often, wondered what it would be like. Now you know. It's good.

Michael licks you again and again, making the cotton even wetter. You can feel everything through the thin, wet fabric. The sensations are getting stronger, more shivery. He starts licking harder, nibbling a little—it's almost too much. A small moan breaks out of you. The feeling is so strong. It almost hurts—but it feels good, too, so good. It goes on, and on, and on. He keeps licking and sucking and nibbling. You want to come, but you can't seem to get there. You're twisting on the bed, arching your back. Then he's pulling your soaked panties aside, putting his mouth right on you, on your naked clit. That almost shoots you over the edge, but it's still not enough. You're not getting there; it feels so good, but you're never going to get there, never going to go up and over the top; you're just going to squirm there, help-lessly, forever. It's driving you crazy, right around the bend—you want to say something, but you don't know what, you can't think straight. His mouth is moving on you so fast, and your lower body feels like a huge puddle of sensations, so many and so varied that you can't keep track of them, you're dissolving, you're losing yourself. That's when Michael puts his big hand on you, too, his hand on your pussy, and a thick finger slides into you, up and in, slick and hard and fast, pushing you up and finally over that edge, his mouth still moving on you as you explode, losing the room, Michael, even your body, everything burning up into a bright shuddering blur that is like nothing you have ever felt before.

"Well, isn't this a pretty little scene."

• PLEASE TURN TO PAGE 147.

That whole thing with Peter was a fiasco. You still don't understand how it all went so wrong so fast. You spend a few weeks sulking in your apartment, working enough to pay the bills but otherwise just holing up in your room, reading cheap romance novels from the grocery store. Listening to Tori Amos CDs on infinite repeat. Your roommates put up with this for a while, then start pushing you to do stuff with them. Group dinners. Clothes shopping with Rose, antiquing with Jamie. Lounging around with Michael—it's what he seems to do best. He's not all that interesting, but he *is* decorative. Your life could be worse. Rose even gets you to go on a couple of dates with friends of hers; she seems to have an infinite supply of friends, and only some of them are also ex-lovers. You've sworn off those, for now at least. None of the dates have gone particularly well, but they haven't been awful, either. In fact, you're going to go on a second date with one of them tonight, a male stripper Rose knows from the sex-worker scene. Astonishingly, he's not gay. He's intimidatingly buff, though: he spends hours working out every day. You're not sure he's all that interested in you, or your body. But he did ask for another date, so what the hell.

You're almost finished getting ready. Rose insisted on your borrowing a dark red dress from her—you'd never have picked it for yourself, but it actually looks surprisingly good on you. And it makes you feel a little scandalous. You're clean, your lipstick's on, and you just need to pull on your heels when the buzzer rings. Stripper-guy is early, it looks like. Michael hollers down the hall: "Got it!" You pull on your shoes, check your face one last time, then walk out of your room, through the kitchen to the hall. What you see, at the end of the hall, makes you stop. You can't take another step. You're not sure you can breathe.

"Hello, Katie."

It's not Stripper-guy. It's John. John walking down the hall toward you, hesitantly. John reaching out, taking your cold hands in his, then letting them go again when you fail to respond. He starts talking; you can barely take it in.

"I'm sorry I didn't call first. I don't know what I was thinking. I wasn't thinking, not really. I was so confused when you left, I just buried myself in work. I worked until bedtime, and then I got up and worked some more. The law firm is going great. But I couldn't work hard enough to block you out; I couldn't stop thinking about you. God, Katie—I missed you so much. You look incredible. Even better than I remembered, and I didn't think that was possible. I finally couldn't stand it anymore, I just drove to the airport and bought a red-eye ticket to San Francisco. I didn't pack anything; I slept in my clothes, and I'm grubby and repulsive and you look so great and I don't know why I thought I might have a chance to bring you back home with me, but I had to try, Katie. I couldn't give up without trying."

• PLEASE TURN TO PAGE 140.

You start to unbutton your shirt—and then you decide to leave it on. Instead, you pull off your panties, slipping them over your heeled boots, which you also leave on. They're not really dominatrix boots, and your loose, flowing skirt isn't black leather, but you're dressed and he's naked, and that's not a bad way of establishing who's in charge here.

He's such a pretty package, all tied up for you. Long and lean and dark and gorgeous. You're not sure what to start with—there are so many toys. What would it be like to whip somebody, to lay into him with a riding crop? Maybe you'd better start with the paddle. You don't want to go all crazy here.

"Roll over." You say it roughly and give his hip a shove. He twists, awkwardly but obediently, and manages to roll over on the bed. Now he's facedown, his cheek pressed against the sheets, his soft cock buried beneath him. Will spanking him get it hard? You're about to find out.

You climb up onto the bed, kneeling next to him. You push some of the unnecessary paraphernalia out of the way. What's it like to be him, not knowing what's coming next? It must be a rush, being helpless, waiting to see what'll happen next. You pick up the paddle, start to bring it down gently, and then stop yourself. What's with the gentle bit? It's a paddle, damn it—it's not meant for gentle. You pull your arm back and then bring it down hard, slapping it against one firm ass-cheek. Peter yelps, and even through the gag, you can hear him. It turns you on, hearing him make noise. He's usually very quiet during sex—part of the whole privacy thing with him. Maybe you can get him to be loud enough that the neighbors hear him. That'd be something. You hit him again, and again, harder.

No sounds. He must have just been startled that first time. You hit him as hard as you can with the paddle, but you get nothing from him. Though his ass *is* starting to redden, even under that dark skin. You pause for a minute, slip a finger under your skirt, and slide it up into your pussy.

- *If you're really enjoying this, if you're dripping and want more,* PLEASE TURN TO PAGE 133.

- *If you're wondering what Peter thinks of all this,* PLEASE TURN TO PAGE 168.

You take his hand in yours deliberately, and he stops talking mid-sentence. You don't know what to say—and this isn't really about talking, is it? You reach out with your other hand, touch his cheek, turn his face toward you again. He looks fragile, scared. You lean forward then, bring your lips gently to his. For a moment, he doesn't respond—then he's kissing you back. Lips closed, kissing you sweetly, and it almost feels like you're children again, kissing in the playground after school. But then his mouth opens, just a little, and yours does, too, and he leans forward, his hand on yours, pulling you closer, then letting go so that both his hands can come up to your hair, tangling in it and tugging gently, pulling you even closer, and the kiss deepens, your body slides forward on the bench until it's pressed up against his, your breasts in their bra and T-shirt just touching the heavy fabric of his suit jacket, your nipples standing straight up and tingles running right through you.

When you finally disengage, there's no doubt in your mind that you find Jamie plenty attractive. But now that he's actually kissed you, how does he feel? "Good?"

"Very good," he says quietly. "Again?"

"Yes, please." And this time he's the one who leans forward, who starts the kiss. His fingers have wandered down to your neck, his thumbs are tracing tiny circles against the skin of your throat, and you're having trouble breathing. It's not long before your mouths are open, hungrily moving on each other, and he tastes likes spearmint and moonshine mixed together. If Michael's all sunlight, steady and glowing, Jamie's the moon, traveling in orbit, and if you're not careful, you could get drunk on moonshine. Who wants to be careful?

You kiss forever, or, more accurately, until a tiny alarm starts beeping. It's his Palm Pilot, calling him back to the office, and already you know him well enough not to be surprised that he would have an alarm set to tell him when lunch is over. It's painfully geeky, but also oddly charming. You say good-bye and go off to your interview in a blur, filled with a strange muddle of thoughts and sensations. Two guys at once. Two guys! You've never even been interested in having two guys at the same time before, and now you're not merely interested, you've got them! The question is, what are you going to do with them?

You land the job, which is great, and dinner's very nice, but you can't concentrate on much of anything except Michael and Jamie. Peter's there, but he ends up mostly talking with your roommates—you just don't have any attention to spare for him. Michael's sitting on one end of the church pew; Jamie's perched nearby. You're sitting across from them, trying not to stare. What happens now? Are you supposed to be dating them separately? That'd be OK—that'd be good, even. But your mind keeps playing little movies of the two of them, together, with you in the middle. What would that be like? In your head, it's pretty damn incredible. But is that what they want? Dinner passes in a fever of anticipation and confusion.

Afterward, you help Rose wash up, then go to your room. You don't know what else to do—they're in their room, and you don't want to intrude. You sit down on the vast bed, just sit and stare at the door, waiting for something to happen. And then someone knocks.

"Come in," you say, just loud enough. The door opens, and it's Jamie. You're relieved that it's not both of them at once—you don't know how you would have handled that. But you wonder why it's Jamie; did they flip a coin to decide who would come see you tonight? How exactly is this going to work?

He comes in, closing the door behind him, walks over to the bed, and sits down next to you. "So," he says.

"So," you agree. And then he turns and kisses you, his fingers splayed across your cheeks, then sliding down your neck, your arms, and your hands are moving, too, tangling in his fiery hair, pulling his head down to kiss you harder, and you're pulling him down to lie on the bed, the length of his body pressed against you. It feels so strange, kissing a man who is nearly as big as you. He isn't in a suit for once—just a button-down shirt and slacks, and your fingers start unbuttoning his shirt, moving quickly. You want to know what his skin feels like, that pale skin. His hands are tugging on your shirt, and you lift your arms over your head long enough for him to pull it off, leaving you in your bra and blue jeans. You help him pull off his shirt. And then he's gathering you in his arms, pulling you close to hold you for a moment, your hearts thumping together.

That's when Michael opens the door and walks in, closing it quietly behind him.

"Mind if I join in?" Michael's tone is joking, but when you pull out of Jamie's arms long enough to look at him, there's actual uncertainty in his face. You don't think you've seen him uncertain before. It doesn't look right on him—Michael was meant to be certain, sure of himself, a great golden god of a man. So you don't hesitate, saying, "Of course not. Come on in, the water's fine!" Matching his light tone, but holding his eyes so he knows you mean it, you want him there. Jamie reaches out a hand to him, so Michael walks forward, takes his lover's hand, and lets Jamie pull him down onto the bed. He falls on top of you both, squishing you into the mattress, squeezing the breath out of you, before rolling away to rest against your back, a massive warm presence that is strangely comforting. Grounding. Jamie's kisses make you feel like you're dissolving, changing into some odd creature of light and liquid and air. Michael brings you home again, to yourself, to your body. Your body, which is now very definitely reacting to having two sexy men pressed against it.

Your nipples are hard, your pussy is wet. You are suddenly impatient with all this clothing and reach down to undo your jeans. But Michael's broad fingers are there before you, unbuttoning them, unzipping, easing them down, while Jamie reaches to unhook your bra's front clasp, pulling it off your shoulders so that you're now almost naked—only a thin triangle of black lace in front, a thong strap in back. You are by far the most naked one in the room, and that just doesn't seem fair.

"Hey, you two. Strip, please."

"As my lady commands," Jamie says, smiling. He unbuckles his belt, undoes his slacks, and slides them off. The loose silk boxers, too, while his cock rises, surprisingly thick for such a small man. God must have figured he needed something to make up for the lack of height. You roll over onto your back to watch Michael stripping—first a tight white T-shirt that barely covers his large chest, then he's peeling out of his blue jeans. He hadn't bothered to wear underwear, which somehow seems very Michael. Now they're both naked, and you're almost naked, and you're still not sure what's going to happen next.

They're not doing anything. Waiting to see what you want, it looks like. So what do you want? They both seem pretty ready for anything. You could have them separately, one after another. On and on until you're exhausted. Or you could try fucking them both. One guy in your pussy, one in your ass. Not that you've ever even had a guy in your ass before, but it might be good—it might be incredible. But maybe that's rushing things. What you actually want is to see what happens. You don't want to run this show. So all you need to do is start them going again.

"Hey, guys. Come kiss me." And they do. First Michael, tasting sharply minty, then Jamie. While one is kissing your lips, another is kissing your neck, your breasts, sucking on your hard nipples. Jamie's mouth is on your breast, and his fingers reach down inside your panties. He dips a finger into your pussy, circles it around, exploring. Brings the moisture up to your clit and rubs it very gently until you moan. Michael chews on your neck; his fingers dig into your ass and you feel like a toy in his large hands. They're touching each other, too. You weren't sure how you'd feel about that, but as it turns out, you find it exciting. Michael gives you one last kiss and then shifts so he's behind Jamie. You watch Michael's broad hands on Jamie's slightly furred chest, tweaking the nipples that are clearly very sensitive. Jamie's quiet, but you can't miss the catch of his breath, and his mouth moves more urgently on yours. His hands are on your waist, your hips, pulling you close so you can feel the bulge of his cock hard against your waist. Michael's hands are busy behind Jamie—you can't see what he's doing and you don't much care right now. Right now your body is aching, your cunt is opening up and it wants to be filled, it wants a cock inside it and it doesn't much care whose.

"Fuck me?" You look steadily at Jamie when you ask, and he hesitates for just a moment before nodding.

"I haven't done this in a long time," he says.

"I'll tell you if you're getting it wrong." You grin as he reaches for his discarded pants and pulls out a condom. You peel off your panties. Everyone's naked now.

"And if you get it really wrong, I'll take over, sweetheart," Michael says cheerfully.

Jamie grins back. "I don't think that'll be necessary. It's like falling off a bicycle, right?" The condom is on and you're hooking one leg over his and he's sliding inside you, and God, he's thick. He has to take it slow, but you are very wet and he keeps going, sliding in and in until he's buried deep inside you, and it feels fucking amazing.

He starts moving then, slow and steady. His arms wrap tight around you, pulling you close. Your face is buried against his shoulder, and you feel Michael drop a gentle kiss on your head. Jamie's moving in and out, and you're tingling all over—it feels so good, like he's fucking not just your pussy but your whole body somehow. It's never felt like this before—it must be because he's so gorgeously thick, and you want to be fucked like this forever. Michael's silent, just watching you both for now. You don't want him to feel left out, but you really don't have much attention left for anything except the fierce pleasure in your cunt, the way you're being filled up, the brush of skin against your clit, over and over, sending you climbing. You manage to reach out a hand, and Michael takes it, interlacing his fingers with yours. And then Jamie's moving faster, kissing your neck, sucking on it, and you're caught up in his urgency, you're rising up to meet him, arching against him, coming hard again and again and again, dissolving into light, into darkness.

When you come back to yourself, Michael's hand is still entangled with yours.

• PLEASE TURN TO PAGE 209.

What the hell. You came here for adventure, right? You didn't come here to be safe. You whisper "yes" against his mouth, and he pulls you up, still kissing you, gathers your clothes, walks to the door. A little part of you wants to stop and find Rose, tell her you're leaving, but most of you doesn't care. Rose will figure it out. He's handing you your coat, your shoes—you're putting them on while he pulls on pants, a coat, shoes, and you walk to the door, naked under your coat, and this is crazy, this is insane, but you don't care. The shock of the cold air hits you hard, but he's kissing you again, his hands are sliding under the coat long enough to cup your breasts, to squeeze the nipples, and he's whispering in your ear, promising to fuck you long and hard, fuck you like you've never been fucked before, and you want to know what that's like, damn it—you've been a good girl long enough, and now you want to go to the limit, let him push you all the way, fuck you until you scream.

A last remnant of sanity makes you say one thing: "Take me someplace public. Not your place." That should keep things from getting too out of hand, right? You don't quite trust yourself alone with him, in his apartment, where anything could happen. He doesn't say anything—doesn't refuse, but doesn't agree, either. You hope that means yes.

He leads you to a car, climbs in, and starts driving with one hand on the wheel and the other busy between your thighs, a finger flicking your clit, then sliding into your pussy. You slide toward him in the seat and spread your legs to give him better access. You feel like the whore of Babylon, scandalous, shameless. It feels really good, remarkably good. He doesn't make you come—he doesn't let you come. He brings you closer and closer but pulls away just as you're about to come. You're ready to scream with frustration when he finally parks the car and lets you out. You're in front of a small door, lit with a red lamp.

He leads you inside and pays the guy at the door. It's dark inside, a maze of small rooms. People are wandering around—mostly men, but some women, too. In one room, a massive frame holds a naked man, spread-eagled. A woman is whipping him, laying long dark lines across his back while he moans. As you pass through the room, you see that his cock is standing straight up, rock hard. You pass other rooms—in one, a man fucks another in the ass. You can't look away, until you're pulled down the corridor, farther along. In another room, a woman is bound to a table, her wrists tied high above her, her legs spread. A man is bent down, licking her cunt, while another man is cutting bright red lines into her skin with a thin razor blade. Christ!

You enter an empty room, and his hands pull off your coat, leaving you naked and defenseless in just a pair of Rose's high heels. You keep expecting him to ask you what you want, to offer you a chance to leave, but instead, he's lifting one of your wrists into a metal wristband fastened to the wall, then the other, and you're not sure how you got into this, but you're going to need him to get you out. You open your mouth to ask him something—you're not even sure what, but he's already wadding a piece of black silk into your mouth, wrapping another around your head to hold it in place, tying it tightly behind your head. And now another around your eyes, and you're blind, you can't see anything, you can't speak or scream—all you can do is whimper in the back of your throat while his hands move on you, sliding over your naked body, moving gently across your skin.

Maybe he will be gentle with you. Maybe all this is just theater, a little drama. Is that why you let him do this, why you walked out of Carol's house with him and into the night? Why you got into his car, let him bring you here, let him chain you to this wall and gag you so that you can't protest, let him blindfold you so you have no idea what's coming next? What were you thinking when you walked out that door?

You weren't thinking at all, and you're not thinking now, not really. Simply waiting in the dark, moaning as a cool breeze drifts across your body, licking at your still-hard nipples. You're still aroused, still wet, but now you're scared, too. And maybe that makes it better? You hang there, on the wall, waiting for him to come back to you, to touch you, to fuck you, maybe to beat you, to whip you. He might bring a friend down to help; he might bring a dozen men to fuck your cunt, your ass. He could pull you down and force you to suck their cocks, one after another after another. He could leave you here for hours. He could do whatever he wants to you, and you have given up all ability to protest, you have walked away from all your choices, and now your only choice is how you will endure what will come to you here, in this dark dungeon, alone.

THE END

Y ou close your eyes, and before you can change your mind, you lean forward and press your lips against Rose's. She's shorter than you, so you have to bend down a little. You've never had to bend down to kiss anyone before! She smells like cinnamon cloves. Her lips are soft, like you'd imagined, and they press back against yours for a moment, starting to open— before she pulls away.

"Hey!" Rose looks totally startled, her eyes wide.

"Oh God, I'm sorry. I'm sorry!" She *didn't* want you to kiss her. She wasn't hinting at all; you've totally misread things. You've sexually harassed your roommate—what's wrong with you? Rose is going to kick you out of the apartment, throw you out on the street, you'll be lost in San Francisco without a place to live, with the only woman you know in the whole city mad at you. . . . You can't breathe. You really can't.

"Hey, shh. It's OK, really it is." Rose reaches out and pats you gently on the shoulder. "I'm flattered, honestly. And that was a really nice kiss."

A nice kiss? She liked it? You hadn't completely bungled it?

"If you weren't my roommate, I'd be tempted, trust me." Rose is smiling. "But I have a strict policy about not dating roommates. There was one guy I dated, Peter, and it turned into a terrible mess when we broke up. Just not worth going there. But hey, if you're looking, I can introduce you to some nice women I know—Carol Queen's having one of her Queen of Heaven sex parties this Saturday night; some great dykes usually show up there."

"I'm not a dyke—really, I'm not. I like guys!" Dyke—what a terrible word. It sounds so hard, so rough. You aren't a dyke, are you? You have to admit you enjoyed kissing Rose. It felt good, or at least you thought it did. It was such a brief kiss. It was hard to tell.

"Well, so do I. But I like girls, too. Don't you? It seemed like you did." Rose is so blunt, so honest and straightforward, somehow she compels a similar honesty in you.

"I don't know." You take a deep breath before the next admission. "That was the first time I've ever kissed one."

Rose smiles sweetly. She looks even prettier. "Well, then I'm really flattered. Honored, even. Am I the first bisexual you've met?"

"The first bisexual woman, at any rate." Michael is bisexual, too. Does that mean his boyfriend is as well? Is everyone in this city bisexual? Maybe the only straight people left are back in Indiana.

"Look, why don't you come to the party. Meet some lesbians, some bisexuals, see what you think. You might meet someone—and even if you don't, it's a great crowd. Think about it, anyway, OK?"

"OK." Did you just agree to go to a sex party? Was that you?

"Great. We're OK, then?" She sounds so earnest, like she really cares whether you're OK. Maybe she could be a friend, a real girlfriend. That would be nice to have in this strange city. A good friend.

"Yes, we're fine. I *am* sorry about that."

"No biggie. Strange cities do that to a girl. Remind me to tell you what happened to me in Prague sometime. But now we really need to rush, OK?"

"OK." You manage to smile at her. It's going to be all right, but you can't help wishing that it could have been different.

• PLEASE TURN TO PAGE 95.

You're left sitting there, wondering what just happened. How did it all happen so fast? You hadn't loved Michael—you aren't even sure if you liked him. But he was so hot, so sexy, and he hit you like a steamroller.

You aren't sorry. Not really. It'll be a pain to get a new place; it might be hellish. But you've gotten some great sex out of it. Maybe you weren't cut out for roommates—but sex, lots and lots of great sex, well, that isn't so bad.

You'll take a shower, get dressed, go get a paper, and look for apartment listings. There's bound to be someplace. For a young single girl in San Francisco, a girl who isn't afraid to go after what she wants, and to take what she finds—for a girl like that, the city is full of possibilities.

You'll be just fine.

THE END

This is nuts. Waiting on a street corner to have lunch with your gay roommate's boyfriend (who is conveniently also your roommate) so you can ask his permission to fuck his boyfriend. But you can't stop thinking about Michael's gorgeous body—John never had muscles like that. You want Michael something fierce, so here you are, and here Jamie comes.

"Hello, Kathryn. I thought we might eat in the park next door; it's nice and private."

"Sure."

You both brought bag lunches, and as you walk down the block to the park, you could be any normal pair of business friends, going off to find a quiet spot to eat lunch and bitch about the office. You don't even know if Jamie's mad at you for fooling around with Michael—Jamie's so calm, so self-contained, that it's impossible to read him. You've said barely ten words to him since you arrived, and now you're supposed to have a heart-to-heart talk? Your stomach is churning, and you don't really want the chicken salad sandwich you bought on your way here. Once you find a nice bench under a spreading tree and sit down next to Jamie, you start sipping from your bottle of water with no idea what to say. Luckily, he seems willing to start.

"So, this is probably a little strange for you." He's spread a napkin across his lap and is eating his own sandwich—it looks like cheese and tomato. He takes small bites, chews them carefully, swallows. Alternates each bite with a drink of water.

"Yes. Definitely. Pretty darn strange. Honestly, I'm not sure how I ended up here."

He smiles but without looking at you. His attention is fixed on his sandwich. "Michael can have that effect on people—he's pretty overwhelming when he pulls his whole golden boy routine."

"Golden boy?"

"Oh, the wandering around half dressed so you can't help noticing how even his tan is, flexing his muscles when he thinks you're looking at him, that sort of thing. It's not that he's doing it on purpose—I don't think he knows what's going on. But he can't help it; Michael just craves attention."

Jamie's finished his sandwich, and he actually folds up the paper it was wrapped in and puts it back in the bag. He puts the lid back on his water and puts that in the bag, too. He's still not looking at you, he's staring at the grass at his feet. Does he hate you? And what is he saying about Michael? Does Michael fool around with anyone who rolls by? Now you're feeling even more queasy. "Oh."

Jamie glances up at you briefly and smiles reassuringly before returning to his contemplation of the grass. "Hey, that doesn't mean he doesn't like you. Michael likes variety in his sex, and I've seen him go through a lot of people—a *lot* of people. They don't bother me. Not much, anyway. They come and go, y'know? It's hard to take any of them too seriously. But he seems a little different with you, like he really likes you. That's why I appreciate your being willing to come have lunch with me. I need to know what your intentions are. I don't want to see Michael get hurt."

He's saying that he doesn't want to see Michael get hurt, but he's tearing his napkin into tiny shreds. Suddenly you feel bad for even hesitating about having lunch with him. You're fooling around with his boyfriend, and you want to do a lot more of it. The least you can do is have lunch with the poor boy and reassure him. You're going to have to be at least friendly if this is going to have even a chance of working. Not that you're at all sure what "this" is.

"Honestly, I'm not sure what my intentions are." His hands keep going, maybe getting more frantic. The napkin's almost entirely destroyed; pieces are floating down to the ground, landing on his shoes, covering the grass around his feet. On impulse, you reach out with a hand and cover his, stilling their frenetic motion. He freezes, his eyes still fixed on the ground, but he doesn't pull away. "But I don't want to hurt either of you. And if that means you need me to stop fooling around with Michael, I can do that. Just tell me what you want me to do."

Wow—where did that offer come from? You hadn't planned on saying anything like that, but it feels right. Besides, how could you live in that apartment and have sex with Michael if Jamie's unhappy about it? It'd be miserable for you, miserable for Jamie—maybe even miserable for Michael, though you're getting the impression that he's almost oblivious enough to be happy in the midst of all that stress and strain. You want to ask Jamie more about that, about Michael's character. Maybe you'd just be letting yourself in for heartache if you got involved with him—Jamie's clearly accustomed himself to Michael fooling around, but is that something you could handle? You have a hundred questions for Jamie, but right now the ball's in his court. It's all up to him.

Minutes pass in the quiet park. The sun's hot against your skin on the back of your neck, and the dense trees shield you from the city noise. You could almost be alone here, especially with Jamie so silent. Even though it's a warm day, his fingers are cold in your hands, and you want to rub them warmer. Finally he turns to look at you, an oddly vulnerable look in his eyes.

"It's OK with me if you date Michael, as long as you don't *try* to break us up. I love him, you know."

"I know." You squeeze his hands reassuringly. You do know—you've seen how they interact, how Jamie brightens when Michael enters the room. And Michael is sweet with Jamie, tender. You can see why: Jamie's quiet on the surface, but this boy has depths, clearly. You're about to say something reassuring, but then you realize he's not done yet.

"And I was wondering . . ." He hesitates, almost drawing his hands out of yours, but then consciously stopping, resting them there.

"Yes?" You rub a thumb gently across two of his knuckles, slow, calm strokes. He has incredibly soft skin, delicate and smooth.

"I was wondering if you'd like to have dinner sometime. Just us. I find you very attractive, Kathryn."

What did he say? Now it's your turn to freeze, to glance up at him and then away at the grass. You're so startled that you drop his hands, pull away slightly—you can't help it. But he's clearly taking it as a rejection; you can almost feel him shutting down. He's talking again, saying something about how he's sorry, how he didn't mean to make you uncomfortable, you should just pretend he didn't say anything. You barely take it in—you're too busy thinking about the idea of dating Jamie. He finds you very attractive! The question is, do you find him attractive? Do you like him?

He isn't really the kind of guy you'd thought of as your type before. John was pretty tall, and Michael is both tall and muscled. Even Peter, the guy at the coffee shop to whom you reacted so strongly, was tall. Jamie's slender, and only a few inches taller than you. His skin is very pale, and with his dark red hair he looks almost like a Irish sprite out of your old fairy-tale books. His eyes are a pleasant green, but his features aren't particularly striking— you probably never would have noticed him at a party. But still, you'd kind of liked holding his hand, touching his skin. What would it be like to touch more of it, to have him touching you? He's so much smaller than the other guys; would it be like touching a guy at all? He's almost androgynous, barely male. Is that something you could be attracted to?

- *If Jamie isn't really your type, and you just want Michael,* PLEASE TURN TO PAGE 163.

- *If you're interested in trying out Jamie,* PLEASE TURN TO PAGE 26.

First one bus, then a subway—what Rose calls BART—to the Powell Street stop. It all goes by in a blur; you're having trouble keeping track of where you are. You end up downtown in a classy mall, and it feels just like the malls at home; you and your mom used to go into Indianapolis to shop every month or so. You see a Gap, and an Express, and feel obscurely comforted. But Rose pulls you past all of those and into a Victoria's Secret, a store you've never had the nerve to enter back home. You'd always bought your underthings at Penney's—wasn't that good enough?

"Now, you'll need to get her exact size. . . ." Rose is talking to a salesgirl, a sharply dressed girl with a long pink measuring tape around her neck. The girl is nodding, and then she's guiding you into a dressing room, coming in with you. The room is large; there's plenty of room for both of you. It's also very pink.

"I'll need you to take off your shirt and bra, to find your exact measurements."

Is this normal? Do women really come in here and get their chests measured? She must be used to women looking confused. She goes on to explain, "Most women are wearing the wrong size of bra; the first step to comfort and beauty in a bra is knowing exactly what size you are." Well, that makes sense. You'd always figured you were a 34C, but maybe . . . . You pull off your shirt and unhook your bra, keeping your eyes fixed on the floor, the wall, anywhere but the girl.

She's strapping the tape around your breasts at various points, chattering about the right way to measure size. It's all very professional, almost like a medical examination. You relax a little. "OK, that's it—you're a 34D. It's a slightly unusual size, but we carry several styles in that. Would you like me to bring you some? What colors are you looking for?"

"Um, sure. Black? And maybe white?"

"No problem."

You pull your bra back on—it's a little silly, since you'll just be taking it off again, but you can't stand around with your breasts hanging out. As the salesgirl leaves, Rose comes in, carrying a big pile of bras, corsets, and panties.

"34D, right?"

"Right." How did she know? Was she looking at you that closely?

"Great! Here, try this on."

She hands you a lacy red bra, very thin. No wires, nothing practical—it's clearly meant to be sexy, even slutty. It's not you, but do you really want to be you anymore? Isn't that why you left Indiana?

• PLEASE TURN TO PAGE 63.

"I'm sorry, I think this is all too complicated for me. Thanks for taking the time to talk to me about it, and I definitely do want us to be friends. I'd love to go antiquing sometime. But I think I'm going to have to leave Michael to you and look for my own man." You shrug apologetically.

Jamie nods, looking relieved. "Michael will be disappointed, but he'll cope. Thanks for talking, Kathryn."

"No problem." You both stand up, and you give him a quick hug. Then he starts walking back toward his office, and you start walking in the other direction, heading back to the apartment. You think maybe you'll call your mother. You miss her voice. And after that, you have a job interview to go to—that's probably a better area to concentrate on for now. You don't need all kinds of relationship complications right now; you just arrived, after all. Tonight's that dinner with Peter, who seems much more suitable. This is clearly the sensible, practical choice—all your friends back home would agree. Heck, they would have thought you were nuts for even considering any of this Michael-Jamie nonsense.

Still, it might have been interesting.

• PLEASE TURN TO PAGE 61.

You force yourself to take a deep breath and smile at Michael. You're determined to give this place a fair shot, despite the snails and jellyfish. He smiles back before leading you down the hall. You move quickly past Rose's room (a mess, bright clothes tossed everywhere), the room he shares with Jamie (scrupulously clean and neat, the way your mother always wanted your room to be), an oddly split bathroom—toilet in one small room, sink and shower in another—and finally into a spacious kitchen. It's almost as big as your mother's. A very rickety-looking dining table sits against a sunny window, flanked by three chairs.

"We usually just pull some chairs into the living room when we have a lot of company . . ."

But before you can comment, he's pulling open a closed door: "Ta-da!"

This must be your room. You walk in—there's a dresser, a nightstand and lamp, a wooden chair holding a folded green quilt, and a perfectly huge bed, covered with fresh white sheets. It takes up most of the room.

Michael walks in behind you, grinning. "Isn't the bed fabulous? There was a couple here before you—they were both fairly large people, y'know? They had the bed custom-made; it's not just big, it's incredibly solid. We heard them banging around on it a lot, but they never broke it. It doesn't even creak."

Michael lets himself fall onto the bed, thumping down and bouncing up slightly. "Amazing springs. You have to try it. No, don't sit—fall!"

What the heck? You lean forward and fall onto the enormous bed. It feels wonderful beneath you, strong and springy and just soft enough. You bounce up and down a few times, feeling like an excited little girl. Then you roll over—and find yourself pressed up against Michael, your arms trapped against his bare chest.

"Well, hello," he says softly. He tilts his head forward and kisses you. His kiss is not slobbery. It is dry and warm, like sunshine against your lips. His free arm comes around you, gently pulling you a little closer. Your heart beats so hard he must be able to feel it. What is he doing? He's gay! More importantly, what are you doing? He has a *boyfriend,* and you're not the kind of girl to try and break up a relationship. But his kiss feels good—really, really good. It's already sent tingles down past your collarbone; if you keep going, how far will it reach? Maybe to your toes?

• *If you keep kissing Michael,* PLEASE TURN TO PAGE 18.

• *If you pull away,* PLEASE TURN TO PAGE 113.

You've gone this far—why not keep going? You're so far now from the girl from Indiana that you don't even think she'd recognize you. You lift your hips and he pulls the pajamas down, where they puddle on the floor, leaving you naked from the waist down. Michael's fingers move to the juncture where you're already wet and wanting him. He goes slowly enough that by the time his thick finger slides into you, you're aching for him, or for something, at least, something to fill you up, to press against the soft inner walls, to curl up, pressing gently against that place you can't reach yourself, the one that makes you want to melt, to dissolve.

You're both leaning forward, each pressing up against the tiny table, and your hand is still clasped in his; your forehead has tipped forward to meet his. It's an intimate position—from the tabletop up, you look like any young couple in love, at a café perhaps. But under the table his towel has fallen away and your other hand has found his muscled thigh, reached out, and taken his hard length. Your hand is encircling it, slowly pumping it there, under the table in this sunlit kitchen. His fingers slide in and out of your pussy, your cunt, in the same rhythm, slow and firm and endless. Your eyes are closed and you're biting your lip—not hard enough to draw blood, not quite. His legs are between yours now, pushing yours apart, wider and wider in this space under the table. Another finger, and another. Three thick fingers in you, pushing you apart, opening you up. And his cock under your hand, the tip wet and slick, the moisture in your hand rubbing up and down his shaft.

Then another finger—or his thumb? Sliding down, down to

your ass, pressing against the entrance there, pausing, waiting for an indication . . .

- *If you want his thumb in your ass*, PLEASE TURN TO PAGE 158.

- *If you don't want to go there (or don't want him to go there)*, PLEASE TURN TO PAGE 111.

You lean forward and slide your fingers into his, interlacing with them. And before he can say anything else, you take it further. Your bare foot meets his, slides up his firm calf and thigh, comes to nestle between his legs. He's not naked, but there's only a towel wrapped around his waist, as it turns out. Your foot slides easily underneath the cloth folds, along the naked flesh. Your toes touch his balls, gently. Michael's eyes widen, and his hand closes around yours, but he doesn't say a word. Encouraged, you continue. Your toes stroke his balls, as delicately as they can. They find the base of his cock and slide along the length, already hardening. You bet it can get harder, though. You slide them up and down—it's a little awkward, and what you really want to do is get your hands on him, or maybe even your mouth, but then he'd be touching you, too, and right now, it's a little intoxicating, touching him, watching him get more and more aroused across the rickety dining table. Knowing that you can do this to him with just your toes.

It goes on for a long time, and it must be enough of an answer, because Michael doesn't mention Jamie again. When your toes finally stop moving, he reaches down and captures your foot in his big hands. He starts massaging your toes, then the ball of your foot, the heel. He digs softly into your calf through the flannel of your pajamas, working the muscles there. He pulls you toward him until you're on the edge of your chair, barely balanced. He leans forward, reaches farther underneath, working his way up your thigh. He pauses there and tugs at your pajama bottoms. He wants you to let him pull them down, here, in the kitchen, where either Jamie or Rose could walk in any minute. Shit—should you be doing this, here, in the kitchen? Even in San Francisco, is this kind of sex OK?

- *If you let Michael pull your pants down,* PLEASE TURN TO PAGE 49.

- *If you don't want to take off your pants in the kitchen,* PLEASE TURN TO PAGE 156.

Dinner is chicken soup with noodles, as it turns out. Before you finish peeling the onions, Michael and Jamie come out of the bedroom. Jamie takes over the cooking, and you end up sitting at the table with Michael, listening to the couple chatter. You can't tell if Jamie knows that Michael kissed you—he doesn't give you any sign that he's angry, or even annoyed. Instead, Jamie teases Michael affectionately; Michael seems to catch only half the jokes, but he doesn't appear to mind. They're comfortable together, a tight unit; they've obviously been together a long time. Watching them makes you want to go hide in your room—but that would be rude. The soup is delicious, with ginger, cinnamon bark, star anise, coriander seeds, bean sprouts, and a very weird sauce whose name you can't spell. Weird but tasty. Still, your stomach feels queasy during dinner and afterward, and when the meal is over, you politely make your excuses and go straight to bed. At least you fall asleep easily, exhausted from a long strange day. You dream about sex—about strangers seducing you in the dark, about two, four, six hands moving across your skin. You wake up in the morning still aroused, with your hand buried between your damp thighs.

This was part of why you left John—no matter how many nights you spent in his bed, you never really felt satisfied. You kept thinking about all the things you'd read about in Sally's letters, in stories you found on the Net. You kept wanting to try things that would have horrified John. At night, you'd lie in his bed after he'd fallen asleep, and you'd touch yourself, imagining what it would be like to have a man's cock in your mouth, in your ass. Imagining being fucked outside, in the grass, or even just up against a wall. Imagining what it would be like to be tied up, blindfolded, gagged. What it might be like to kiss another woman. John just followed the same old routine, every time, kissing and touching and then good old missionary-style intercourse. You knew there was so much more out there, so much more that your body wanted to try, but you'd never had the nerve to ask John for those things. You knew how he'd react if you did.

Someone knocks loudly on your door—and then pushes it open, without waiting to hear you call. You pull your hand out quickly, grateful for the heavy quilt.

→

"Hey, chica!" It's Rose, a little more dressed than yesterday. This time she's wearing a white button-down shirt with the sleeves rolled up. Nothing else that you can see, but at least it reaches down to mid-thigh. It's sort of like a nightshirt.

She bounces onto your bed, talking at top speed. "Sorry to barge in like this, but I need to go out for a couple of hours, and I wanted to make plans for later. What if we meet up here at lunchtime? Two-ish? We can go shopping then, and be at the club by six?"

"That sounds fine. . . ." You're not sure what time it is now. Eight? Nine? Too early. Did you actually agree to go to this strip club with Rose? You don't remember agreeing, but why not at least visit? It'll be educational. Besides, she's so enthusiastic; it's hard to resist.

"Great. I'm gonna go shower now—there's juice on the counter and toast in the toaster. Nutella, too. You like Nutella? European hazelnut spread—it's amazing, especially if you stuff a banana into your sandwich. Just one thing—we're out of coffee. Sorry! Jamie'll go shopping later today; in the meantime, there's a coffee shop on the corner, Café International. I've heard their coffee is pretty decent—I'm not a coffee drinker myself, so I can't swear to it. OK, gotta run!" And she's gone again. You rub your eyes, wondering if you imagined her entirely. It's hard to think clearly. Coffee. You need coffee.

You stumble out of bed, pull on underwear, a sweater and jeans, socks, sneakers. You pull your hair back into a ponytail—maybe it won't be as obvious that you haven't washed it yet. You grab your wallet and keys, heading out the door. Coffee.

• PLEASE TURN TO PAGE 217.

It almost gets to be a game with the two of you—how much further can you go? He still won't do anything in public, but aside from that, you haven't hit any barriers yet. You keep pushing each other—a little further, a little faster. He takes photos of you naked. You rent a video camera and tape the two of you having sex. It doesn't look as attractive as you'd hoped, but it's kind of sexy anyway. You give each other a lot of oral sex, and you get pretty good at sixty-nine. At first, it had been too distracting, and you'd been afraid you'd bite his cock when you got excited, but eventually you got the knack of it. You're learning to deep-throat him, and that's a different kind of exciting—it doesn't hurt, but it's kind of scary, not being able to breathe with a cock in your throat. One of the smutty books he buys you says that you can learn to breathe around it, but you haven't figured out how yet. You're still trying, though.

You start wondering about some of the other things in the books, the kinkier stuff. So far, everything you've done has been pretty harmless—just about sensations, pleasant ones. But a lot of the stories have at least an edge of pain to them. Anal sex. Nipple clamps. Spanking. In the stories, the pain makes the pleasure more intense, and you wonder if it actually works that way. One night after a really good fucking, when you're both lying exhausted on his dining table, you hint to Peter that you're kind of interested in experimenting with the S&M stuff, and he gets a funny look on his face. You can't quite tell if he's turned on by the idea or weirded out. He doesn't say anything, just pulls you close and kisses you. Kisses you until you forget all about the S&M stuff and drag him to the bedroom for some more comfortable sex. Dining tables are all well and good, but they don't have a lot of give to them.

The next night, you unlock the door (he gave you a key the second week you were dating) and come in, calling his name. You find him in the bedroom, naked, his wrists crisscrossed and strapped to the headboard with soft, fur-lined black leather cuffs. The bed is strewn with a bewildering array of toys: nipple clamps, a paddle, a short whip, what looks like a riding crop, a dildo that would be small for a pussy but pretty big for an ass, lube, and a pile of leather straps—that must be a harness for you to wear. He's blindfolded and gagged. He can't have done all this himself; he must have gotten a friend to help him. He had to tell somebody about all of this; that must have been hard for him. What does that mean? Does that mean that he really wants this, this hard-core S&M stuff? And what the hell do you do about it?

- *If you decide to just go along with it and see what happens*, PLEASE TURN TO PAGE 24.

- *If you decide to stop and make him talk to you first*, PLEASE TURN TO PAGE 167.

He's definitely hot, but you're not the kind to break up a relationship, even a gay one. You wouldn't even know how to start. Besides, the thought of trying to take over from a gay guy, who would know *exactly* what to do in bed to make his lover very, very happy—that's scary. You'd better stick to what you know: straight men. And maybe women?

But enough thinking about sex—you're starting to feel a little obsessed with it. What you need right now is money, if you actually want to stay in this city. And getting money means finding a job.

"So, that job you mentioned?"

"Well, it's entry-level, so the pay's not that great—only twenty-five dollars an hour."

That's not great? That's amazing. But maybe not here? You try to figure out in your head how much that'll leave you after taxes and rent, but it gets too complicated.

"You'd be working with several other writers, putting together a user manual for some genealogy software. Easy stuff—they give you time on the job to learn the software, and then it's just a matter of writing down the steps."

That doesn't sound too bad. You've certainly complained plenty about other user manuals—it'd be great to get the chance to do one right.

"It's only a three-month gig, but if they like your work, they'll probably hire you for other projects. The best part is that you'd be working from home, meeting with the rest of the team online. They'll loan you a computer if you don't have one of your own. We have a cable modem setup here; if you want to use it, chip in ten bucks a month."

It all sounds great, especially the bit where you get to work in your pajamas all day. You could go days without ever leaving the apartment! You agree to go to the interview at three.

"Good morning, Kathryn." Jamie walks into the room, leans down, and gives Michael a quick kiss before stepping over to the coffeemaker. You step back, out of his way, but not quite quickly enough—his hand brushes yours, and an electric spark jumps through you, shooting straight down to your pussy. You have to fight to keep a calm expression—what's wrong with you? Jamie's cute, but not that cute! Are you going to react this way to everybody you meet in this city? If so, you'd better find someone who's single and available before you go turning into a rabid sex maniac! You take a deep breath and step farther back. Jamie fills his cup, apparently without noticing any sparks. He smiles at you as he takes a long drink of his coffee. "I'm sorry I can't stay and chat, but I overslept a bit today. Have to run . . ."" Another long swig, and then he's rinsing out his mug and is gone down the hall before you have a chance to say two words to him.

"Oh, and remember," Michael says as he stands up (revealing that he is, in fact, only wearing a towel, which looks dangerously close to slipping off), "roommate dinner tonight. We try to all eat together on Friday nights, and guests are welcome—you just need to let Rose know. She usually makes spinach lasagna—it's totally yummy."

"I don't actually know anyone here to invite yet." You really need to meet people. You can't be spending all your time with your roommates. Maybe at work . . .

"Well, you will soon. Peter will probably be here—he's Rose's ex, and he comes most weeks."

Peter. The sexy chess player. Somehow, in all the time you were fantasizing about him, you'd managed not to think about the fact that he knew your roommates already and that he'd dated one of them. "Her ex? Is it going to be tense?"

Michael nods slowly. "It was a tough breakup; they'd been pretty serious about each other for a while. Totally in love but couldn't make the whole long-term, babies, marriage, etc., thing work. Jamie and I have that all planned already. Well, mostly he planned it, but I signed all the papers."

"Oh?"

"Yup—we've got an adoption application in. It'll take a while, but someday."

Now you're really glad you didn't try to interfere with their relationship. They're going to be parents! At least your mother would like that—she loves babies.

"Anyway, Pete and Rose are good friends again now. Pete's a good guy. No worries."

He gives you an encouraging pat on the shoulder, sending shivers right through you, and then turns and walks back down the hall to his bedroom. You go back to your own room; you're feeling a sudden urge to call your mother.

➤

Ypou curl up in your bed and dial the number. It's strange, dialing the area code for your mother's house. She doesn't pick up until the seventh or eighth ring. "Hello?"

"Hi, it's me. Kathryn. Sorry I didn't call sooner—it's been really hectic here."

"That's all right, dear. It's been busy here, too. You wouldn't believe what Ellen's daughter has been getting up to." And she's off, telling you some long, boring story with barely a hint of scandal. If she only knew the things that were going through her own daughter's head. Eventually she runs out of story and remembers to ask, "So, how are you settling in?"

"Oh, fine. My roommate Rose is a sweetheart."

"What does she do?"

"She's a grad student at Berkeley, in psychology." Truth, just not the whole truth. But at least you didn't have to outright lie.

"Well, that's nice. Is she seeing anyone?"

You should have known that would be the next question. "I'm not sure, Mom."

"Well, maybe she knows some nice boys she can introduce you to. You're not getting any younger, you know. I still don't understand why John wasn't good enough for you. He was such a nice boy."

And now you're remembering why you didn't feel like calling your mother right away. What's most frustrating about it all is that it's not like she has the perfect marriage she so badly wants you to have—your father took off to find himself a decade ago, leaving her to raise you by yourself. You'd think she would've learned something from that. But it's not a subject she'll discuss with you. You learned long ago not to even try. Instead, you shift the conversation to the weather. You don't mention the peep show, or the male roommates, or the gay roommates, or the upcoming sex party. There are some things your mother doesn't need, or want, to know. When you finally get off the phone, you feel both comforted and frustrated. That's just about right for conversations with your mother.

By two, you're ready to go, in blue jeans and a light sweater. You feel totally underdressed for an interview, but Michael said it would be appropriate. You've decided to walk—it's sunny out, and as you walk up and down the hilly streets, admiring the painted ladies, the old Victorian houses, you can imagine staying here for a long time. The city is a little grubby, but in a very friendly way. By the time you reach the interview address, you've fallen in love with at least three houses along the way—tall buildings with turrets and cheerful paint. You really want that job!

As it turns out, the interview is nothing like what you expected. The building turns out to be a house, the home of the lead writer. She talks to you for ten minutes, takes one quick look at your résumé, then pronounces that "you'll do." She leads you into the back of the house, where six other people sit around a kitchen table piled high with pizza. This is the rest of the team, as it turns out, and before you know it, you're sitting down with a slice of chicken-pesto pizza and a thick style manual in front you. Three hours later, you're walking home, a little dazed but happy. You're a tech writer! In San Francisco!

• PLEASE TURN TO PAGE 82.

You turn a little, take off your old bra, and try on the new one. When you look at yourself in the mirror, you look strange to yourself, like a different woman. Older, but in a good way. You look experienced, maybe a bit dangerous. The kind of woman who might leave the lights on, who might have mirrors on her ceiling—or a box of sex toys under the bed. You don't own any sex toys; maybe you should buy some. Rose must know where to go for them.

Would Michael like this on you? You shouldn't be thinking about that, but you can't help imagining the look in his eyes; your thighs are tense and your nipples are hard, pressing noticeably through the thin fabric.

"Hey, that looks great—really hot! What do you think of this?"

Rose has skimmed out of her clothes—you've never seen anyone undress so quickly. She's topless, wearing a tiny little black lace panty, with thin straps that go over her hips and a triangle of fabric that barely covers her. She's either shaved or so closely trimmed that you can't see anything around the panties. You've never shaved down there—are you supposed to? You do your armpits and legs, but do you really want to shave there? Maybe it would feel good? Maybe it would be fun?

"It looks really nice." Nice isn't the word, but what are you supposed to say? Can you tell another woman that she looks sexy, delectable? She does, but you can't say *that*. . . .

Rose grins. "'Nice' isn't exactly what I'm looking for, but I suppose it'll do." She pirouettes slowly in the room, considering herself in the mirrors. Her breasts are impossible to ignore—small but firm, with large dark aureoles and thick nipples. Yours aren't nearly that firm, but they're much fuller than hers. She's looking at yours with approval, though. "The guys are going to love those breasts. Maybe you want a push-up, so they're kind of spilling out?"

"Sure—I can try it, anyway." You can try anything. What would it hurt? No one will ever know what you do in this little dressing room—just you and Rose. You can be whomever you want; the red bra is like a costume, turning you into someone else entirely.

The salesgirl knocks on the door, and you pull it open enough to take the bras she hands you. Rose is trying on a black ribbed corset that pushes up her breasts. As you turn to put the bras down, you bump into her, knocking her off balance. She stumbles, and her breasts bump into your arm. Her breasts! You've never touched another woman's breasts before. "Oh, sorry! God, I'm sorry. . . ."

"No, no, it's OK." She's smiling at you, only a few inches away from you. She doesn't seem mad; her eyes are sparkling. "You're cute when you're embarrassed, you know?"

She's not hitting on you, is she? Is she a lesbian? Why would she work as a stripper if she's a lesbian? Your face feels incredibly hot; you're probably blushing bright red. Her mouth is slightly open; her lips look like they want to be kissed. You could kiss her—it wouldn't kill you. You've never even thought about kissing a woman before—what's going on with you? Should you do it? What would it feel like? Would it be softer than kissing a guy? Sweeter?

• *If you kiss Rose*, PLEASE TURN TO PAGE 36.

• *If you don't kiss her*, PLEASE TURN TO PAGE 229.

You take a more cautious sip from your coffee—and then spoon a little sugar into it. Maybe black coffee is an experience you have to get to in stages. And speaking of experiences . . .

"So, about the other day. Do you have to kiss all your roommates?" You slide into a chair opposite Michael. His bare knees bump against yours; unfortunately, you're wearing flannel pajamas. They had seemed like a sensible choice given the morning chill, but maybe boxers and a sweatshirt would have been enough. Or maybe boxers and a tank top. Or maybe nothing at all—you can't seem to take your eyes off his naked chest. Your fingers are itching with the desire to touch him.

He pauses before responding, as if he's figuring out exactly how to put what he's about to say. "Well, Rose and I have had a few nights here and there, but Jamie isn't attracted to her, so we gave it up after a while. Then she had that mess with Peter, and now she's kind of nuts on the whole topic of roommates dating. Hates the idea. You can't talk to her about it. She's OK with me and Jamie, since we were together before we moved in here— but she doesn't make much sense on the subject."

That wasn't much of an explanation; maybe he should have thought longer before explaining. "Um, I'm confused. You dated Rose? I thought you were gay!"

"I'm bi. I've probably had as many girlfriends as boyfriends before Jamie and I hooked up. Jamie's mostly gay, though even he's been known to slide over the line on occasion. That was how we met, actually—over a woman's body."

"Really?" Now you're intrigued.

"I was seeing this girl, Karina—really gorgeous. Looked a little like you, actually: blond hair, blue eyes, very nice curves. Though her hair went all the way down to her ass. She was an Australian chick; I met her over the net, in this newsgroup, soc.bi. Karina was only in the States for a few weeks, but I'd offered her a place to stay in San Francisco, and it wasn't long before we hooked up. We met Jamie at the Folsom Street Fair. He was volunteering in a kissing booth, raising money for some charity."

"That's sweet." You can't quite picture Jamie in a kissing booth, but it's a charming idea.

"Jamie's big into that kind of volunteer thing. So anyway, they kissed, they liked kissing and wanted to do some more of it, she brought him back to my place, I walked in on them, joined in, we screwed like bunnies all night . . . and then she left for Melbourne the next day, leaving me and Jamie to console ourselves with each other. Not that Jamie would have been likely to stay involved with her—he's never been with a woman for more than a night. I think he just hasn't met the right woman."

"Okay, but I'm still confused." More and more confused, in fact. "I get that you started out in this sexual three-way fling, but I thought you guys were a couple now." And couples are supposed to be monogamous—aren't they?

"We are a couple, definitely. And see, Jamie's an intense, true-love kind of guy. He likes being settled down and doesn't miss his flinging days. Me, I like playing around." Michael shrugs, raising his hands in the air. He looks endearingly helpless—and almost painfully charming. You can see why Jamie might find him hard to resist.

"Jamie-boy will put up with a little bit of my wandering, as long as I keep coming back to him. I always tell him about it, usually in advance. You just caught me by surprise." Michael grins.

"I caught *you* by surprise?" Michael thinks you came on to him! Did you? You'd thought you understood what had happened in the bedroom, but now you're not sure.

"Well, rolling up to me like that. Don't get me wrong—it was really nice. I liked it. I'd like to do it again, if you're willing." He reaches out to stroke a finger lightly over the back of your hand. It feels strange, like tiny ants crawling across your skin. It's warm in here.

"Is Jamie willing?" You had to ask that, right? Even though part of you wants to drag the big golden boy back to your bedroom with its massive bed and never mind the damned boyfriend.

"Does that matter to you?" He's pulled his finger back and is looking straight at you, not smiling now.

Do you care what Jamie thinks of all this? The old Kathryn would have cared. She, along with her mother, her aunts, and her best girlfriends would have thought that any woman who'd steal another woman's man was the lowest of the low. Another man's man was the same thing, right? But Michael's eyes are locked on yours, and his hand is just an inch away.

• *If you care what Jamie thinks of all this,* PLEASE TURN TO PAGE 162.

• *If you really don't care what happens to Jamie,* PLEASE TURN TO PAGE 51.

Up a few steps to another door, which is unlocked and slightly ajar. You hope they don't always leave it that way. Rose did know when you were supposed to arrive, roughly. Maybe she left it open for you? You climb the stairs, your heavy duffel slung over your shoulder. The stairs aren't very well lit—if there is a light in the stairwell, it's burned out. The carpet on the stairs is dingy, stained. It smells acrid, sharp. Like a toilet. Has someone been urinating in your stairwell?

One flight, two flights, three flights, four. You pause for a second on the fourth landing, close your eyes, and catch your breath. Just one more flight to your new home. You feel dizzy—you haven't eaten anything yet today, and you've been sitting on a bus for days. In a few more steps, you'll have to face your new roommates, your new life. You're leaning against the wall when a dark stranger comes hurtling down the stairs, slamming into you. Your arms come up reflexively, catch his lean body, steadying him. His body feels kind of nice, pressed against yours for just a moment before he pulls away.

"Hey—sorry about that! Are you OK?" He's tall, at least six feet. Very dark-skinned, too, almost blue-black, or at least it looks that way in the dim light of the stairwell. Sharp cheekbones, dark eyes.

"I'm fine, don't worry." And you are fine, not even bruised. But your heart's beating a little faster. You smile reassuringly at him. He smiles back.

"There's a loose step on the next flight—I still trip on it every time. You should watch out for it."

Every time? Is he Rose's boyfriend? "I'm Kathryn, the new

roommate." You stick out a hand, determined to be friendly. You're going to need friends out here.

He shakes your hand. "Peter." He grins then, an amazing flash of bright white teeth, making you immediately self-conscious; you haven't flossed since you left Indiana. The bus-stop bathrooms were just too disgusting to spend much time in. "Rose's ex. Nice to meet you. I'll see you at Friday dinner. Gotta run—I'm late for class, and if I don't get there by ten after, the students assume I'm not coming and take off."

Students? He's a professor? He doesn't look old enough. But before you can ask, Peter's gone, his long legs moving too quickly down the rickety stairs. No wonder he tripped. A part of you wants to follow him, talk to him a little longer. Or maybe not just talk. But you have roommates to meet. You start climbing the last flight of stairs.

The door at the top is open.

• PLEASE TURN TO PAGE 15.

You can't quite believe you're doing this. Standing outside what looks like a normal house in a normal city neighborhood, wearing a long coat, and nothing under it but a pale blue bra and panties and a white button-down shirt, mostly unbuttoned. Plus heels, which you plan to take off as soon as you get inside. Rose had informed you that sexy clothing was mandatory at Carol's parties—lingerie, fetish wear—or you could always go naked. You could see how that might help break the ice, but God, it was unnerving. Rose is actually wearing more than you are—a Catholic-schoolgirl outfit—white button-down shirt with a loose black tie, short red plaid skirt, black knee-high socks, saddle shoes. Her hair tightly braided into two plaits, the tips hanging down just over her nipples. No bra, no underwear. If she bends over at all, you'll see bare ass. Lastly, a gold cross on a thin gold chain around her neck. She said that by the end of the night, she plans on that being the only thing she's still wearing.

Carol opens the door and invites you in, greeting Rose enthusiastically. She's an attractive woman with a sleek cap of silvery blond hair framing her face and heavy black glasses, very hip, perched on her nose. She looks like someone's favorite teacher. She ushers you into the main room, where everyone else is gathered. Apparently, you two are the last to arrive; this is strictly a private party, and Carol's been checking people off the guest list as they come in. She and her partner, Robert, step into the center of the room and welcome everyone, running briefly over the rules: no alcohol, ask before you touch, stop immediately when asked, and everyone practices safe sex here, regardless of what they might be doing at home. Condoms, dental dams, and gloves are scattered around the room, along with lots of pillows. The lighting is soft, and music is quietly playing in the background. It's a very mellow setting, though some of the forty or so people are clearly nervous, giggling a little too hard when Carol makes a joke. You're controlling your own desire to giggle, but it's difficult. What would your mother think of forty grown men and women dressing up in skimpy clothes and coming together to have a lot of slippery sex? Such a concept doesn't enter your mother's world. And that's enough thinking about your mother—she doesn't belong in this world, either.

Carol leads you through what she calls a ritual. You pair up, sitting on the floor facing each other, and raise your hands to almost meet those of your partner. Rose's hands are a tiny bit smaller than yours; she's smiling encouragingly as you hesitantly match palms. As it turns out, the ritual is an exercise you used to do in theater back in college, as part of warm-ups: you take turns being the leader, moving your palms, while your partner tries to match you. It takes focus, paying attention. It can be a lot of fun, but it's not particularly sexual. Or at least, it never has been before.

Somehow here, in this setting, with all these half-dressed people and Carol's soothing, sexy voice instructing you, with Rose's eyes intent on yours, it gets sexy. Very sexy. The hair on your arms is tingling, and the tingle is spreading up your arms, along your skin to your breasts where they rub against the pale lace of the bra, sparking at your nipples. Rose is leading down, pushing her hand toward you while you pull yours back, barely not touching, tilting it so that it skims over your shoulder, then down the valley between your breasts. Then the control slides to you, and you continue the motion, sliding down to your thighs, cross-legged and bare, then across to Rose, up to circle infinitely slowly around a breast. And you realize that you're getting aroused, and you're not sure if it's the ritual or if it's Rose. Do you want to explore what it would be like, to be sexual with a woman? Or is this all weirding you out too much? The ritual is ending—what do you want to do next?

• *If you want to approach Rose for something more*, PLEASE TURN TO PAGE 100.

• *If you want someone else, someone male*, PLEASE TURN TO PAGE 179.

You smile. "I'm not particularly into it; it was only something Rose suggested. To be honest, I'd rather have dinner with you." There—that was pretty unambiguous. Bold, even. Peter seems to like you bold, though; he's smiling broadly now. You could melt into that smile.

"That's great. I'll take you someplace special." He's leaning in close; you can feel the warmth of his body radiating across to yours, and your pussy is creaming in your jeans. You suddenly wonder if he can smell your arousal. You can certainly smell him, though you can't place the scent. Slightly spicy, very male. Breathing him in makes you dizzy.

"It doesn't have to be anyplace fancy . . ." You hesitate, then decide to come clean. "To be honest, I don't have any of my dress-up clothes yet anyway. I just came here with one duffel bag."

Peter nods solemnly, still grinning. "Special, not fancy. Trust me. I'll pick you up at six? We'll be eating in Berkeley, so it'll take us a little while to get across the Bay."

"Sure, six is great." Six is fabulous, six is perfect. Five would be even better. Or you could invite him to stay the night—no, no. You don't want to rush things and turn him off or make Rose angry. Dinner tomorrow.

"Great. Tell the others I said bye, OK? I'll see you then." He bends down, rather awkwardly. For a minute, you think he's going to kiss your cheek, but then he swerves slightly, and his lips are pressed to yours. A spark runs right through you, and you can't help letting out a tiny whimper. Peter's lips are firm. One of his hands cups your cheek, and your own hands move up to press against the soft fabric of his shirt. You feel like you're melting—the only solid point in your body is the intersection of your lips with his. Before you're ready, he pulls away, grinning. "Excellent. Can't wait for tomorrow!" Then he opens the door and walks through, letting it swing shut behind him. You lean against the wall, dizzy.

• PLEASE TURN TO PAGE 115.

No, you're overreacting. OK, so you got a little carried away. This is all new, it's understandable. Michael is certainly nothing like John—you weren't prepared for a guy with so much sex appeal. And hey, it's not like he's all about sex. He went to get a condom, so he's considerate, too. Even in Indiana, there were plenty of guys who didn't want to use condoms, who pressured their girlfriends to do it without them. Two of your high school friends got pregnant (and quickly married) that way. John probably would've pushed you, too, if he hadn't been such a limp noodle of a man. Guys are apparently different in San Francisco—sweeter, smarter. Or maybe it's just gay men who are more considerate. Maybe they have to be.

Michael slips back into the room, foil packet in hand. He closes and locks the door behind him, and then pulls down his towel. Wow. He's even larger than your toes had thought; now you're a little worried that he won't fit inside you. But he's tearing open the packet, rolling the rubber down over his hard shaft, and moving up onto the bed, all before you can quite catch your breath. This guy moves fast! His hands are sliding up your naked body; his mouth is moving, hot and wet and eager against your skin. Your head is falling back onto the bed, your eyes are closing, and this time you don't need his hands to push your legs apart—you spread them wide yourself, tilting your pelvis up and inviting him in, your hands on his body urging him up. And he's there, the tip of his cock thick and hard against your pussy, then sliding in, and God yes, you can take it—it's stretching you wide but you can take it in, and it feels so good. Your nails dig into his back, begging for more. You can't quite breathe, but it doesn't matter; he just keeps going and going and going, inch by slow inch until he's finally buried inside you, buried deep, and the breath goes out of him in a sigh that is by God the sexiest sound you've ever heard. And then he starts to move.

So slow, so slow you want to scream. But even with the door closed, you can bet Jamie and Rose would hear a scream, so you muffle the sound deep in your throat, closing your mouth against his thick shoulder muscles, and when he thrusts into you, you bite down, whimpering. He doesn't make another sound, just slides silently in and out, his cheek pressed against the top of your hands. Your bodies arching together, pressed so close that you can't breathe separately—you take silent gasping breaths together. Your legs wrap around his, and you're barely touching the bed; with each slow thrust, you're pushing your bodies a little closer together, sweat-slick making your grip slippery, but you don't let go. You can smell him—you can't smell anything else. Just a delicious sweat, late summer in the cornfields. God damn. Jesus fucking Christ. It's pure blasphemy, what you're thinking, what you're feeling, but you don't care, it doesn't matter—nothing matters but this slow pounding, this glorious pulse riding you, rising through you, filling you up until you can't contain it anymore—it's spilling out of you, soaking into the sheets, and leaving you lost and trembling, cradled in Michael's strong arms.

When you're done, he rolls you both over, and you rest, falling asleep against his massive chest, still breathing in slow synchronicity.

→

You wake up alone. The alarm clock shows that you weren't asleep long, maybe half an hour. Long enough for Michael to disappear, though. You feel a brief twinge of—something. Distress? Uncertainty? You're not sure. Everything's gotten so scrambled since you arrived in this city. You just had mind-bending sex with a man you met two days ago, a man who already has a long-term partner. It was amazing, and you'd certainly like to do it again. Over and over. You want him back in your bed, you want him holding you, cuddling you, just talking to you—you wouldn't mind doing that for the rest of the day. Maybe he's even a guy you could learn to love. He seems sweet enough. But he's not yours—or at best, not *only* yours.

Michael has a boyfriend, and you have no indication that he's going to be leaving Jamie for you. He's had sex with women before; you're not going to convert him to heterosexuality just because you had some great sex. Hell, maybe it wasn't even great for him. You don't have any idea. Maybe he's back in bed with Jamie right now, telling him what a disappointment you were, saying how glad he is to be back with a real man. Shit. Can you handle this?

It's going to be pretty hard to tell from this bed. You swing yourself out and pull on your pajamas again, wincing at the soreness between your thighs. If you're going to be having sex with Michael often, you're going to have to get used to being sore. Or maybe your body will adapt—you're not sure. You walk over to the door and lean your head against it for a minute. It's a lot to take in. What'll be on the other side of that door? Michael, waiting for you? An empty apartment? Jamie, with hurt eyes? Jamie, with a kitchen knife in his hand, waiting for you?

You're overreacting again—you think. But whether you are or not, at some point, you're going to have to open that door and walk through it. Might as well be now.

• PLEASE TURN TO PAGE 138.

"**H**onestly, Peter, I was really looking forward to the party. It sounds like it'll be a blast." You're about to suggest getting together later in the week, for a more normal first date, but he cuts you off.

"Well, I'm sorry to hear that, Kathryn. It's not my kind of thing." His forehead is all scrunched up; he looks disgusted. "I guess maybe we're not so well suited after all. Friends?" He's holding out a hand to shake, waiting for you to take it.

Well, shit. Peter's just a big prude, isn't he? "Sure, friends." You shake his hand, disappointed. You're sad not to be going on a date, but you're more disappointed in him—you'd expected more from him, somehow. Maybe because he was Rose's ex, you'd thought he'd be more adventurous, more exciting. Maybe now you know why they broke up—'cause he's plain old boring. You say good night and shut the door behind him. You go to bed, hoping that tomorrow will bring something more interesting.

• PLEASE TURN TO PAGE 224.

Yiou lean forward and pull the curtain closed, giving yourself a minute alone, just a minute to take it all in. You're wearing nothing but heels and stockings, working in a peep show, and you haven't been in San Francisco even a week. And you're enjoying it. It's a rush, a power trip. These men want you—they need you. They're giving you a lot of money. And you're doing things you've never done before. That last guy, you'd almost wanted to let him touch you. And what would that have been like?

But the longer you lie here with the curtains pulled, the less money you make. So you pull your panties back up your legs and hips. You put your bra back on. You turn to face the hallway window, tuck your legs demurely under you, and pull the curtain open.

There's a man standing right there, waiting for you.

You're startled but manage an inviting smile. You're not trying to look seductive, just friendly. If you're going to make it in this business, you need to work with what you have, and what you have is a nice girl-next-door, fresh-off-the-farm sort of look. You know it. You look sweet. And judging by the two guys you just got off, it's working for you. The new guy comes in; you switch the curtains, enclosing you both in a private space. He says, "I'd like to watch you fuck yourself—"

Same as the last guy, no problem. You're getting to be a pro at masturbating for men. Though that's an odd way to put it, to fuck yourself . . .

"—with a big, fat dildo." He gets the last words out in a rush, in one breath. And then he takes another breath and throws out some more words: "With a butt plug up your ass."

Wow. You'd been briefed on this kind of thing. There are some toys in a box in the back of the room that you can use, along with a bunch of condoms to put over them. You're supposed to charge a fair bit more to put on that kind of show. You've never used a dildo, and you've definitely never had anything up your ass. Not even a finger! You could just say no and let the guy walk away. They said that was OK, if you didn't turn down too many of them.

- *If you go for it,* PLEASE TURN TO PAGE 86.

- *If you turn him down,* PLEASE TURN TO PAGE 102.

Yget home to find Rose the only one there. She's sitting in the kitchen, sipping a cup of what smells like peppermint tea. She looks lovely, in a dark red dress, and you wonder if you should have dressed up more. Not that you have anything that dressy with you. You really need to have your mother send more of your clothes!

"Hola, chica. There's a pot of tea on the stove—why don't you pour yourself a mug?" The counter holds the ingredients for lasagna: frozen spinach, ricotta, mozzarella, sauce, noodles. Your stomach rumbles quietly.

You pour a mugful and sip a little. It's very minty. "You look beautiful." She does, with her dark hair falling in waves down her back, her slender legs crossed, her feet in gorgeous sparkly heels. She smells good, too, a hint of something floral—jasmine?

"Thanks, you're sweet." Rose gets up and puts the spinach in a dish and sticks it in the microwave to start thawing. "I try to dress up a little when Peter's coming; you want to look your best for your ex, y'know? Make him sorry you got away." She pulls a large pan out of the oven and opens a box of noodles.

You're not sure what to say. You don't know how much you like Peter, but you know you like him. You're not sure if he's interested in you; you could ask, though. You've never asked a guy out, but maybe now would be a good time to start. But it could be messy if Rose is still carrying a torch for him. "Are you sorry you guys broke up?"

Rose shrugs slightly as she pulls the spinach out of the beeping microwave. "Here, help me squeeze the water out of this." You obediently take handfuls of soggy spinach and squeeze them hard, standing beside her over the sink. She smells even nicer up close.

"Peter and I never would have worked. He can be a lot of fun; he likes trying new things." Rose frowns at the spinach for a moment. "If you can finish this, I'll get the rest of the stuff ready."

"No problem." You can squeeze spinach.

Rose rinses her hands, then opens a jar of pasta sauce and dumps it in a bowl, adding some water. She stirs it slowly, mixing it in. "The boy likes a little adventure—he really dug the interracial thing. Dating a girl his papa wouldn't approve of, that gave him a kick. But there's only so far you can push him; there are things he just flat out refuses to consider. Threesomes, for example. I like an occasional threesome. With Peter, it was all about the twosome, y'know?"

That doesn't sound so bad to you—you're pretty sure you're more the twosome kind yourself. Anything else just seems too complicated. Hell, if you'd wanted complicated, you would've gone after Michael.

Rose opens the ricotta and peels back the film. "Deep down, Peter's the marrying kind. If I'd stayed with him, I'd have had to turn monogamous, which has never been my thing. And probably have a couple kids. Kids are fine, but for other people. Not for me."

What a weird idea. Back in Indiana, every woman you knew had just assumed that she was going to have kids. It wasn't even a question.

Rose starts layering noodles in the pan. "Peter and I broke up two years ago. We've both dated other people since then. It's really no big deal." She's glopping on ricotta and spreading it smooth, layering spinach, then sauce, then mozzarella.

You rinse the leftover spinach bits off your hands and step back. There doesn't seem to be much else for you to do here. Rose starts the second layer of noodles, ricotta. Which leaves you plenty of time to think about Peter—his sharp cheekbones, his slender hands. The thought of those hands on your ass, pulling you close to him, makes your legs wobbly. "So you wouldn't mind if I asked him out?"

"Asked him out?" Rose is so startled that she stops her smooth layering, ricotta still clinging to the spoon in her hand. "But you haven't even met him yet."

"Oh, I met him already." It's embarrassing to admit—it feels almost as if you were scheming, trying to deceive Rose. But it had just happened . . . "The day I arrived, in the stairwell. And then I ran into him at the café. I think he's pretty cute."

"Oh, he's definitely cute. No doubt about that." She goes back to layering—spinach, sauce, mozzarella. "It'd be a little weird if you two got hot and heavy." She adds one final layer of noodles, a little mozzarella, a little spinach, and a drizzle of sauce. It's a beautiful lasagna. "It might be better if you didn't have sex with him here. He's got his own apartment, no roommates there. You could just boink at his place." She covers the pan with foil and slides it into the oven.

"That'd be fine." You're relieved at such a simple solution. If she's really OK with the dating, then keeping the sex out of this apartment isn't such a restriction. If there is any sex. "But we're not really at the sex stage yet. I don't even know if he likes me." You smile hesitantly at Rose.

Rose grins, picking up her mug of tea. "Well, we'll just have to find out, won't we? But maybe you should take some time to freshen up." She sips from the tea, then reaches out and pats you gently on the shoulder. Even that simple touch sends a little shiver through you. "Go on now—shoo. And go ahead and use my cranberry-vanilla bath scrub; it's yummy. Drives the boys wild."

You feel guilty leaving Rose with the cooking dishes, but there's really not that much to clean. And after all that walking up and down the hills, you could certainly use a long, hot shower yourself. Maybe, if you're very quiet, you can work off a little of that sexual tension, too.

• PLEASE TURN TO PAGE 121.

You didn't come to San Francisco to be a chicken. "Sure, no problem. But that'll be fifty dollars for the dildo, and another fifty for the butt plug." Is he really going to pay a hundred dollars just to watch you do this? But it seems that he is: he pulls five twenties out of his wallet and pushes them through the slot. He's got a lot more in there, too—you wonder how much you could've asked for. You really need to talk to Rose about standard rates at this job! But that's for later. Right now you need to stick a piece of silicone up your ass.

You pull the box out of the back corner of the room and open it up. There's a variety of toys in there, and you quickly grab the smallest item, which looks like it's probably a butt plug. It's about as long as your middle finger, though at least twice as thick, with a flared body and a flat base. You'll pick the dildo later; right now you need to figure out how to get this in you. You quickly open a condom and put it on, then pull a bottle of lube from the box, which should make you nice and slippery. You hope. Can you hurt yourself doing this?

You could still back out, but you're not going to. Instead, you peel off your panties, lean back on the cushions, the box open to your right, and spread your legs wide, giving him a good view. You're not thinking about him now. You're putting some lube on your right forefinger—you figure you're going to have to start with a finger if you hope to get the plug in. You take a deep breath, close your eyes, and bring the finger down to gently caress your asshole.

It feels—strange. Strange, but not bad. Kind of shivery. You rub your finger gently against the tight hole and feel goose bumps all over your skin. You'd like to just do this for a while and get used to the sensation, but the longer you take, the less you're going to make tonight. So in it has to go. You bite your lip, and then press your finger against your asshole. To your surprise, your finger slides in easily. Without pushing hard at all, you're already in, up to your second knuckle. And it feels even better inside than it does on the surface. You tentatively pull it out, slowly, and can't help whimpering at the intense sensation. You push your finger back in—it's just as strong, just as good. Out and in again, a few more times, and you can feel your body tensing, wanting more, wanting something longer and thicker. It'd be a little scary, letting a guy fuck you there, but now you can see why it might be fun, too. But right now you don't have a guy. You have a silicone plug, sheathed in rubber. That'll have to do.

You slide your finger out, shivering again. It's such a weird feeling. You open your eyes long enough to lube up the plug, then close them again as you bring the plug to your asshole. It's harder to push in than your finger—it's thicker even at the tip, and once you get that in, you have to kind of work the rest in, pushing it in and pulling it out, trying to relax and take it in, breathing deeply. You're gasping a bit with the effort, and you have no idea what's going on with the guy on the other side of the glass, but it doesn't matter. Whether he's enjoying the show or not, you're enjoying it—it feels better and better, as the slick plug slides up into your ass, pushing farther each time until finally, with a hard push, it goes all the way in and settles, pushed flat up against your ass. You feel incredibly full, and when you squeeze your butt muscles, you get those same shivery sensations again. It feels really good, but you're not going to come from this. You want more. Luckily, he wants more, too. . . .

One toy in, one to go. You pick a small dildo out of the box and sheathe it in rubber as well—God knows how many women it's been in. You oil it up, carefully rubbing lube all over it. This shouldn't be so bad—it's about the same size as John's cock. You can take that. Some of the other dildos are much longer or thicker or both, and you wonder if there are actually guys shaped like that. If there are, you need to find one! But for now you'll stick with what you know. There have to be limits on how much new stuff one woman can do in one day. Even Angela.

The plug is tight and your ass is very sensitive to it; every inch of it pressing against you feels good, feels sexy. And now you're pressing the slick dildo against your wet pussy, pressing it in easily, pulling it out again. Oh, God. It's almost too much—when it's deep in there, you can feel it pressing against the other side of the wall that the butt plug is on. You feel so full—it's hard to take, almost too intense. You push in again, slowly. Your left hand squeezes a nipple briefly, and it's like an electric shock, running through you. You bring that hand down to your clit, but for a moment you're almost afraid to touch yourself. You've never felt anything like this, nothing even close. You slide the dildo out, and then in, and then out again. Your leg muscles have tensed up; your body is arching off the pillows—you can't help it. Then the plug starts to slide out, and you slam yourself back down again, shoving it back into you, and you groan with how good it feels. A low, dark growl, animal, a sound you've never heard before.

He makes a sound, too, but you don't care. This isn't about him anymore—it's about the cock you're fucking yourself with, the plug up your ass, your fingers now touching your clit, rubbing not gently—rubbing hard, fucking hard, and your body twisting on the pillows, on the platform, whimpering. Fucking in and out, harder and harder until your arm is aching, your fingers are getting sore and so is your cunt, but you don't care, you want more and more and you can't feel anything separately anymore—not ass or pussy or clit. You're just one pulsing mass of sensation, one shivering skin enclosing a wave rising higher and higher, carrying you up until finally, finally you explode, flooding the sheets, banging your head hard against the platform.

You're a mess. You've made a mess, and the plug has slid out of you, the dildo, too. You ache all over. But you feel incredible—utterly sated. You want to do it again.

• PLEASE TURN TO PAGE 17.

You grab a towel and wrap it around yourself hastily before dashing out the door and down the hall to your bedroom, dripping water on the wood floors. Luckily, you don't pass anyone on the way; the kitchen's empty. Once in your room, you towel off your body and your hair, glad that it's not long anymore—long hair was sort of fun, but this is so much faster. The alarm clock says 8:05—you were in the shower quite a while! You quickly pull on the black lace underwear; no one's going to see it, but you'll know it's there. A pair of fitted blue jeans, a tight black sweater that shows off your curves. Barefoot would be sexy, but also cold. Black socks instead—you don't need shoes. A quick finger-comb of your hair and you're ready to go; casual but hopefully appealing. You were never much good with makeup, so if Peter's going to like you, he'll have to like you without it. Deep breath. Go.

When you come out into the kitchen, it's still empty, but you can smell the lasagna from the far room, and hear quiet laughter. You walk down the long hallway, past the other bedrooms. The apartment is oddly dark; the hallway light is off. When you reach the living room, you find out why—the room is filled with candles. Tall wrought-iron pillars in the corner hold an assortment of thick creamy candles, the battered wooden coffee table boasts a scattering of tea lights in frosted glass cups, the fireplace is full of fat round candles, and around the room, in nooks and crannies, various other candles burn cheerfully. It's not quite the same as a roaring Midwest fire, but it's surprisingly warm. And gorgeous. You didn't know the apartment could look so good. The lasagna looks delectable, paired with a massive bowl of salad and a long loaf of crusty bread. Two bottles of red wine, wineglasses, plates, and forks sit waiting, and your stomach rumbles loudly. You're blushing again.

Rose grins from where she's perched on a windowsill, almost hidden by a large ficus tree. "Guess that's our signal to eat! Kathryn, you know Peter already, right?"

Peter smiles at you from where he leans on some cushions at the near end of the church pew; Michael's sitting at the other end, and the two of them, tall in the candlelight, look like paired angels, bright and dark. "We've met. It's good to see you again, Kathryn." His voice is sexier than you remember. Maybe the noise of the coffeehouse had drowned it out. It's low and deep—he must be a baritone at least, maybe even a bass. The sound of it thrums through you. The shower took the edge off, but you're clearly not completely satisfied yet. If you were, you wouldn't be standing here, almost dazed, wanting to walk over and take Peter's hand in yours, or bend down and kiss him, or crawl into his lap.

"Good to see you, too, Peter. Sorry I kept you guys waiting." You smile apologetically at them all, but especially at Jamie, standing in the corner and frowning slightly.

"No, no, the lasagna needed to sit for a few minutes anyway." Rose gestures to the plates. "You go ahead and start—you're the newest one. Hope you like it."

"I'm sure it'll be wonderful." The phrase slips automatically from your lips—it's a good thing your mother trained you to be polite no matter what, because you're really not paying much attention to anything but Peter. You're fighting not to stare as you serve yourself, as you sit down in a battered love seat, as you sip your red wine. It's tasty—thick and rich. You almost don't need to eat. But you'd better. The lasagna's good. Though right now your mind is elsewhere. Peter's talking again, and you try to listen to what he's saying—some story about grading student exams—but it's so hard to concentrate. What would it be like to have him whispering in your ear, whispering words of love—or maybe dirty words? Both sound good; you're not sure which you'd rather have. Maybe you won't need to pick—he seems like the kind of guy who could be romantic *and* sexy. You'd heard there were guys like that out there.

He's looking at you, too, and smiling. Your eyes keep glancing over to him only to find his eyes on you. You're not saying much, but he doesn't seem to mind. When you finish your first glass of wine, he reaches out and pours you another without interrupting Jamie, who's telling some complicated story about rummage sales. You've tuned out entirely. Peter's fingers brush yours on the wine-glass, and you bite your lip, glancing down. If you looked at him, he would surely see the naked desire in your eyes, and that would be a bit much for a first dinner.

The evening passes in a swirl of conversation, laughter, wine. You even tell a story or two yourself—the others seem to find the antics of small-town life in Indiana endlessly amusing, which is good, 'cause you can tell those stories forever. There are plenty of them. You tell the one about the three cows and your cousin Jimmy. The one about the crazy postman and the big red gate. You even tell them about the time when your mom went to the minister's house for dinner and found his wife in a very compromising position. And then it's gotten late, very late, and Jamie's clearing the plates and Rose, kind Rose, is asking Michael to help her in the kitchen, leaving you standing alone with Peter, alone in the living room in the light of the guttering candles.

It's awkward for a moment, quiet. Then you manage to speak. "I had a really good time tonight. This was a lot of fun." You look up at him, smile. You know you have a good smile, a girl-next-door smile. If you can get a guy at all, it's with that smile.

Peter nods. "They're a great group of people. Lots of fun."

What does that mean? That's a vague comment. Does he like you? Have you been reading him wrong all night? Hell, maybe he already has a girlfriend. Surely Rose would have said something. But maybe she didn't know? Maybe he just doesn't like you. Maybe when you thought he was looking at you, he was actually looking next to you, at Rose in the windowsill. Maybe he still loves her. Is he interested in you at all?

You've never really asked a guy out. If he says no, it'll be really embarrassing. Especially since he comes here for dinner every Friday night. But you do like him. He's smart, sweet, and oh so cute. And he laughs at your stories—that's a good sign, right? You want to go out with him, but he doesn't seem like he's going to make the first move. It's going to be up to you.

• *If you ask Peter out,* PLEASE TURN TO PAGE 98.

• *If you find it too difficult to ask a guy out,* PLEASE TURN TO PAGE 223.

Some of this was interesting, some of it was even fun—but some of it was just plain weird and uncomfortable. You're glad you tried it, but you don't want to be doing this for your daily bread. There have to be better ways to earn your rent money.

You make your way down the hall, just missing bumping into a pair of breasts as you go. The hallways are dingy, the walls are sticky, and even though you don't have to pass any men to get to the dressing room, the thought of them out there, so hungry and lonely, is depressing. Your heel catches in a gummy spot on the threadbare carpet, and you can't help thinking longingly about a nice clean office, brightly lit, humming with happy computers. First thing in the morning, you're going to talk to Mike about that job.

• PLEASE TURN TO PAGE 142.

Y<span></span>ou finish shopping, buying three new bras (red, black, and pale blue) with matching panties, two pairs of black thigh-high stockings and a lacy black garter belt, and a sheer black nightgown with thin straps; it falls to your ankles and is slit up one side to mid-thigh. You stop quickly at Payless and pick up a pair of black stiletto heels—you can't afford good boots right now. Maybe soon. Even if you don't get a job stripping, it can't hurt to have this sort of stuff. Trying it on made you feel sexy; wearing it at home will probably make you feel even sexier. The pale blue set isn't quite as sexy, but it's sheer, and somehow you look very innocent in it. Rose took one look at the set and said you looked good enough to eat, and that's good enough for you.

It's gotten late, so you jump on another bus, heading up to the Lusty Lady. By the time you arrive, it's dark, and the street is lit up with neon signs, outlines of naked women, "XXX Video," "Adult Video." The Lusty Lady itself advertises "Live Nude Dancing" and "Private Booths," "24 Hours." You don't have time to look around, though; Rose pulls you inside and signs you in at the desk.

"She's with me, Steve." Steve smiles at you—it's a friendly smile, not a leer. "OK, Carla. No cameras, remember."

"Carla?" You're confused.

Rose says, "We all have stage names. I'm Carla while I'm here, OK? I should've told you earlier. Who do you want to be?"

You consider using Sally's name for a minute, but that would be too weird. "How's Angela?" Angela was the girl in fifth grade who everyone said was putting out. Angela would do anything under the bleachers. So they said, anyway.

"That's good, perfect. Names that end in an 'a' are sexier. Steve, can we have some quarters for the booth? Angela's here for amateur night, and I want to show her around."

Steve reaches under the counter and pulls out some quarters, handing them to Rose. She leads you farther into the club to a set of doors.

"OK, so first, grab some tissues." There's a dispenser on the wall, and you help yourselves. "You don't want to touch anything in here, trust me. Not *anything*." It takes you a minute to understand why; when you do, your stomach churns. She opens the door with tissues in her hand, and you step into the booth. It's a corner booth, larger than the others. Wheelchair accessible? Maybe.

Rose puts a quarter into the slot, and a dark window slides open, leaving a layer of Plexiglas between you and the stage. You're a little below stage-level, looking up at a brightly lit room where two women are immediately visible. As you edge farther in, a third comes into view. Rose is talking, explaining the routine, the rates, but you're barely taking that in—you're only able to focus on the dancers.

One is slender, dressed in red panties, high heels, a red boa. She's leaning against a wall, her hips gyrating slowly. She looks a bit bored. Another is a brunette, her attention focused on another window; she's wearing a leather belt, black panties, and cowboy boots. She's leaning forward, touching her breasts, squeezing her nipples for the man on the other side of the glass. The third woman is black and much curvier than the other two. You're surprised—you would have thought she'd be too heavy to be a stripper. But she looks really sexy; she's in a sheer black chemise that comes to mid-thigh, and she's naked underneath, with dark nipples and a furry mound clearly visible. So you wouldn't *have* to shave—you're relieved, but a little disappointed, too. You might try it anyway. You can't seem to take your eyes off her; she's standing in the center of the room, her hands sliding up and down her body, gently caressing herself. Her eyes are closed, and she looks completely absorbed in her own pleasure. She's moving her hips and thighs—really her whole body, in a way that you're not sure you can duplicate.

"So, you want to give it a shot? Amateur night starts in fifteen minutes, just enough time to show you the dressing room and get you ready." Rose's tone is very calm, not pressing at all. If you wanted to, you could chicken out right now, turn around and go home, and you're pretty sure Rose would never say a word.

Do you really want to take off your clothes in front of a bunch of strange men (and women)? The only people who've seen your naked adult body are your ex-fiancé and your doctor. And now Rose. The money would probably be really good, but would you enjoy it? Or would it all be too weird?

• *If you decide to give amateur night a try*, PLEASE TURN TO PAGE 9.

• *If you decide this was interesting but not for you*, PLEASE TURN TO PAGE 166.

You say the words quickly, before you can change your mind. "So, Peter—would you like to have dinner sometime?" There, you said it. And that's clearly an invitation to an actual date, considering that you just had dinner. You're having a bit of trouble breathing as you wait for his answer.

"I'd love to," he says quickly. "How about tomorrow?"

Tomorrow! He must like you a lot if he wants to go out tomorrow! But tomorrow's something else. Oh right—Rose had mentioned a sex party while you were lingerie shopping. Maybe he would want to go with you? Is that the sort of thing people do on dates in San Francisco?

"Well, there was this party that Rose wanted me to go to tomorrow . . ."

He frowns slightly. "Not a Queen of Heaven party?"

"Yes, actually. I think that's what she said." It's embarrassing to admit—he obviously knows it's a sex party. Maybe Peter's been to them? But he doesn't look happy about it.

"They're not really my kind of thing—and it's a little much for a first date, don't you think?"

That's a good point. A very good point. Maybe it'd be a bad idea, going to a sex party with someone you haven't even kissed yet. Especially if he doesn't like sex parties. Are *you* into that kind of thing? Do you want to go to a party with a roomful of mostly naked strangers? Do you want to watch them having sex, and let them watch you? Especially if it means giving up a sexy, funny guy, one you could maybe have a future with? You just met Peter a few days ago, but something about him captivates you. He seems like he could be someone special, and he's looking for love, for marriage, for kids eventually. Maybe he could find that with you. Still, the sex party does sound kind of fun— this isn't a choice you want to make, but it looks like it's being thrust upon you.

- *If you want to ditch the sex party and makes plans for Saturday night with Peter,* PLEASE TURN TO PAGE 73.

- *If you're looking forward to getting naked with strangers,* PLEASE TURN TO PAGE 79.

Carol stops talking and moves off center stage. Around the room, some couples are breaking up, some are getting further into it. People have started walking around, talking. Some are heading into the kitchen for snacks. Rose lowers her hands and smiles at you.

"That was really fun," you say. "Thank you."

"Thank you!" she says. "You're good at it—the motion was really smooth." She doesn't make any move to get up; she seems content to stay here, knee to knee with you, talking. The couple next to you must have really gotten into it—they're on the floor now, and out of the corner of your eye, you can see his mouth moving on her breast.

"College theater workshops; we did the same stuff. But it wasn't so sexy." Your voice is trembling. It's embarrassing, but you can't help it. This is all so strange. You have no idea how to hit on a woman, and it's not like you can just lean in and kiss her. This is a sex party—you're supposed to ask first. "Did—did you think it was sexy?"

She looks slightly uncomfortable. "Well, yes. Kathryn, you know I think you're hot. But I really do have a strict policy against dating roommates."

"Rose . . ." You take your courage in both hands. "I'd love it if you kissed me." You lean forward, just a little. Your eyes are locked on hers. All she has to do is lean forward, too, press her lips to yours. So she has a rule against dating roommates—how strict can it be? Isn't this more important, your soft lips, slightly open?

Her eyes widen, looking oddly vulnerable, uncertain. The moment stretches until you're almost ready to give up, almost ready to pull away. But then Rose licks her lips, leans forward, and kisses you. It starts as a peck but quickly softens into something more. God, her lips are so soft. You've never touched lips as soft as hers. You kiss for a long time, then pull apart again.

"See, that wasn't so bad."

"But we're roommates!" It's almost a wail, and her eyes are still wide, almost panicked.

"Can we please worry about that later? I just want to kiss you again. I want to undo that tie. I want to unbutton your shirt." You can't believe you're saying this to a woman, but it's true, you do. There are couples having sex all around you—you think that's even a threesome across the room. Men with women, men with men, women with women, and this is probably going to be your best chance ever to find out what it's actually like to have sex with a woman. Rose is so beautiful—she might be the most beautiful woman you've ever seen. If she can just manage not to chicken out. "Please—give me a kiss tonight, and I promise I won't bother you again after we leave. I just want to know what it's like to make love to a woman."

• PLEASE TURN TO PAGE 198.

Y ou've never actually said no to a guy—it's harder getting the words out than you expected. But you take a deep breath and manage to say, "No. I'm sorry, but I don't do penetration with toys. I can do something else for you, though."

The guy flushes bright red, and for a minute you think maybe he's going to take off. But instead, he takes a deep breath, looks down, and asks, "What can you do?"

Shit. It's up to you now—why do you have to say it? *Can* you say it? What *is* it, anyway? What are you willing to do?

You can at least do the things you've done already, right? That can't be so bad.

"I can dance for you. I can strip for you. I can touch myself. My breasts, my nipples, my pussy. I can come so you can hear me . . ."

He's still looking down, but his hand has crept to his crotch. He's not quite rubbing himself, only resting his hand there, over the suddenly visible bulge. He says softly, "Can you keep talking like that? Talking dirty?"

You guess you can; you just did. It didn't feel dirty. But what are you supposed to say? "Um, sure—but what do you want me to say?"

"Could you just—be my girlfriend? And we're on opposite sides of the country, and you miss me, and want to have sex with me? And you're telling me about it?" He's still not looking at you, his hand frozen over the lump in his pants. It's kind of sad. He looks like he's about forty or so, and something about the way he said "girl-friend" tells you that he's never had one, that the only sex in his life is what he gets coming into places like this. It makes your chest hurt looking at him, so carefully not looking at you, the almost naked girl in the window.

"Sure, honey. Sure. I can do that. But you have to tell me your name."

"Bobby."

"OK, Bobby." You take a deep breath. You can do this. Maybe if you pretend it's John—John the way he should've been. The fiancé so far away, the one you have crazy sex with and hate having to leave. The one you're desperately in love with. The kind of fiancé Angela would have had.

"Hey, Bobby. I've missed you, sweetheart." You drop your voice a little, keep it soft and slow. You lean back on the cushions, close your eyes. It's late at night and you're on the telephone, talking to your honey who is too far away. You can hear his breath, though, thick and uneven through the static on the line. "I miss your hands on me. Unbuttoning my dress, sliding it off. I never wear a bra or panties when I'm with you, so it's just a few buttons and then I'm naked, pressing my body against yours, leaning my hand on your shoulder. I miss the way you touch my shoulder blades, my back, the way you run your fingers down my spine, over my hips."

This guy doesn't just want sex, he wants a girlfriend. "I miss your kisses. The way you kiss me, so softly. Soft at first, and then harder, pulling me up against your chest and hips, against the big bulge in your pants . . ." It's not that big a bulge. But this is his fantasy. "It makes my pussy cream, being pressed up against you like that. And when you lay me down on our bed, in the sunlight, and look at me—God, I feel so beautiful then. Like a princess. But I can't stand it if you just keep looking at me. I need you to touch me, honey. I need your strong hands moving up and down my body. Cupping my breasts and pinching my nipples. I need your fingers sliding into my wet pussy, curling up in that way you know I love. I need your hot, wet mouth on my neck, on my breasts, sucking on my nipples. I love it when you bite down, just a little bit. It sends sparks right through me, and I can't help moaning . . ."

Your breath has gotten heavy—it's sexy, doing this. Strange, but sexy. You really are getting wet again, and you slide your right hand into your panties, curving a finger inside you, moving it in and out, a counterpoint to your voice, to your whimpers and moans.

"But I need more than that, baby. I need you to fuck me. I need you to take off your clothes and push your hard cock deep inside me." That'd be nice right now—a boyfriend with a long, thick cock. But your fingers will have to do. You slide another one in. Now you're pumping two, slowly, in and out, dragging them across your clit before sending them back inside. You're shivering. "Oh, Bobby, baby, sweetheart. I miss you so much. I want you inside me, your hands holding my hips, pumping them up and down. I want your long, thick cock."

He's getting louder, his breath coming fast and hard, and without looking, without opening your eyes, you know that he's about to come—and you'd bet money that his eyes are still closed, that it's simply your voice doing this to him, your breathy voice and the sounds you make. It's an incredible rush, knowing that, and your hand moves faster in your pussy—it feels so good, and you're losing track of what's going on, but you keep going anyway. "Your mouth on mine, kissing me like you're never going to stop. I want your cock, baby, I need it, I need it in me right now. I've got my fingers in my pussy, but it's just not good enough. Oh, baby."

And now you're close, you're close and sliding up and over, you can't talk, you're gasping breaths—but you have to talk. You're just a voice on a phone line, and you can't stop talking. "Oh, I want you to fuck me hard, fuck me so hard, so fast, that I can't think, fuck me until I see stars, until I'm slamming my head against the fucking wall!" And there it is, there you go, coming hard around your hand, and you whimper loud, almost loud enough to drown out the sound of him gasping, of him coming to the sound of your voice. You come and come, and then finally take a deep breath, let your fingers slow down, stop, resting inside your pussy, inside the red lace panties. And you finish the story: "Bobby, love, I want you to fuck me the way you did last week, last week before I had to get on that plane, get on that plane and go so far away from you. I can't wait until I see you again . . ."

When you open your eyes, he's gone. But a crisp hundred-dollar bill has been pushed through the wall slot. He must have gotten what he wanted, even if it wasn't what he came for.

• PLEASE TURN TO PAGE 17.

You gently disentangle your hands from Peter's. He looks down at his water glass, as if he doesn't want you to see his face. He must already know where this is going.

"Peter, I'm sorry—I think you're really cute, and sweet, but I think you and I are looking for different sorts of relationships right now."

"You don't know what I'm looking for." His voice is quiet, bitter. He's taking this way too hard. He just met you a few days ago!

"I'm sorry. I think I do. Now please, would you walk me back to the train? I know how to get home from there."

"Don't be silly. It's not safe—I'll take you home."

And he does. You try to make conversation once or twice on the train, but he's not cooperating, and eventually you give up. Besides, you're hungry from missing dinner—right now you're mostly thinking about what leftovers might be in the fridge. You can grab something quick when you get back; Rose hadn't been planning on leaving until nine-ish. Hopefully the sex party will be more fun than this. Poor guy.

• PLEASE TURN TO PAGE 70.

Before you can fully process that experience, before you can even put your bra back on, another man is walking into the room.

"Hey, you OK?" He's closed the door, sat down. He looks—normal. Like a guy you might meet in a coffee shop. Blue jeans, button-down shirt. "You look kinda dazed."

"Just a little shell-shocked. The last guy was—well, he was weird. It was my first time." You smile weakly at him.

"Sorry it couldn't have been me." He smiles. "I'm Joe."

"I'm Angela, Joe." Introducing yourself as Angela makes it easier. This isn't you sitting up here, being called bitch and cunt. This is Angela, and she isn't real. "What can I do for you?"

"I'd like to watch you touch yourself, if that's OK?" He's friendly, if hesitant.

"That'd be fine." You've never done that in front of anyone before, unless out in the main room of the peep show counted. This feels different, alone with Joe. But you think you can do it. It might even be fun. "Thirty bucks, please."

He pulls the money out of a slim wallet and slides it through the slot. Then he sits back, relaxed, as if he has all the time in the world.

You aren't sure at first how to arrange yourself so he can actually see. If you lean back, you'll have to bend forward to reach, and that probably won't look as good. But he probably doesn't care about that; it's not about the extra folds in your stomach. That's not where his eyes will be. You peel off the red panties, leaving your garter belt and stockings on. You're not quite ready to stick a finger down there, so you start with your breasts, leaning back on the pillows, closing your eyes for a minute. Caressing your breasts lightly, squeezing them, rubbing the nipples. It's not long before you're aroused again, your juices flowing, a moan rising from the back of your throat. You bite it back, embarrassed. John had always told you to be quiet.

"Please," Joe says. "I'd like to hear you."

It's sexy, hearing him say please like that. You can hear it in his voice, the thick desire. He wants to hear the sounds you make. You lick your thumb, rub it across a nipple, let yourself moan. Just a little. It sounds good. Sensual. Wanting.

You slide a hand down, from breasts to waist to flare of hip, sliding inward, coming to rest on your mound, a finger right above your clit. You touch yourself gently. You're wet, the moisture thick on your lips, your clitoris. You rub your forefinger against your clit, whimpering slightly. It feels electric. You rub it back and forth, then slide a finger inside yourself.

"Please, would you mind? May I?"

You open your eyes and he's got his hand on his belt buckle. His eyes meet yours, and you aren't positive, but you think it's a real question. If you say no, then he'll take his hand off his pants and just watch you. But you don't want him to just watch, you want him to participate, as much as he can.

"Go ahead."

You keep rubbing, sliding a finger slowly in and out. He unbuckles his pants and slides them down. He's wearing soft plaid flannel boxers, blue-green. His cock juts out from the opening in front, thick and slightly purple, though maybe that's the light in here. It's not very long, but it looks long enough. You wonder, just for a moment, what a normal guy like this is doing at a peep show. He should be able to get a date. Then he's lubing up his hand from the dispenser on the wall, putting his hand on his cock, encircling it and slowly stroking. Matching his speed to your own finger in your pussy, in your cunt. Looking at you, all of you, not smiling now but still somehow friendly, intent. He's leaning forward, pressing his forehead against the glass, as if he might dive forward, into your cunt.

You spread your legs wider for him, and a sharp thrill rushes through you. He wants you so badly. You're rocking now, rocking your hips to meet the finger, two fingers, that you're thrusting into your cunt. You're moaning louder, and it's only a little bit louder than you might normally moan, it's only a little bit for him. Mostly it's real, it's for you, it's the rush of watching a man watching you, aching for you, biting his lip and sliding his hand up and down a rock-hard cock that is going to come any minute, just from watching you touch yourself, watching you give yourself pleasure. That thought alone is enough to send you up and over the edge, to make you shake and shiver and come and collapse, your finger finally slowing, finally stopping. It's only when you're done that he comes, too, spurting out over his hand, covering himself. More of a gentleman than dumb John had ever been, even if John would rather have been shot dead than admit to visiting strippers.

"Thanks, Angela." He's cleaning up, getting ready to leave, pushing more money through the slot, and you have to ask.

"Joe, why's a nice guy like you—"

"—coming to a place like this? My wife, Sandra—she's great, but she won't let me watch her. I really liked watching you come." His voice is soft, and he's smiling as he turns the knob, walks out, letting the door shut behind him.

It seems kind of sweet, in its own way, though Sandra might not like it if she knew. The whole thing was nice, really. Nice and exciting and in some ways a bigger rush than any sex you've ever had. It took the sting out of the creepy guy. But that doesn't mean they'll mostly be nice; maybe they'll mostly be creeps. You still have time to back out, to give up this rush and take a nice, safe job in an office somewhere. You could find sexy adventures elsewhere in your life—do you really want to be performing sexual acts for money, eight hours a day?

• *If you stay in the booth,* PLEASE TURN TO PAGE 80.

• *If you give up on sex work,* PLEASE TURN TO PAGE 94.

You don't say anything, but you shake your head, just a little. He pauses as if disappointed, but then his thumb moves away. Maybe someday, but right now that's not what you're looking for. Some regular sex would be fine with you.

His thumb dips into your pussy, just long enough to pick up some juices—then it's on your clit, rubbing just hard enough to send waves of piercing pleasure through you while his fingers move deep inside your cunt, curl up to press against your sweet spot, and it feels like you've contracted down until you're nothing but the pleasure from his hand, nothing but a cunt, hot and wet and throbbing, and all you ask is that he not stop. Please don't stop . . .

• PLEASE TURN TO PAGE 235.

Your roommates are sorry to see you go, and you're sad saying good-bye to them, too. It's been only a few days, here in the city, but it's certainly been interesting. You've learned a lot.

Still, maybe there's such a thing as too much experience. Or if not too much, then enough, at least. You feel like you've learned enough. When you get back to Greendale, you won't be trapped in the role of good daughter, good girlfriend, good wife, the role you thought you had to play. Maybe you never had to—maybe it was only you, telling yourself you had to act a certain way. Maybe now, when you talk to your mother and to John, you can tell them how you want to be treated, tell them what you want from life. Maybe you can make a good life for yourself, home in Indiana.

You wouldn't have missed this, not for the world. But as the Greyhound pulls out of the station, you feel a profound sense of relief. This city, this enticing, dangerous city, isn't where you belong. It feels so good to be going home again.

THE END

Y ou pull away, the feel of Michael's lips still hot against yours. You sit up, then stand up. Being on a bed with the man doesn't seem safe. "I can't do this, Michael."

"Hey, hey. Sorry if I misread things. Really." He was sitting up, somehow looking smaller than he had. "I'm always doing that— but you were just so sexy in that little tank top. I'm sorry."

"It's OK. But you have a boyfriend. And you're gay!"

He grins, a little bashfully. "It's still kind of fun kissing girls. Maybe you better think of me as bi."

"Fine." You'd heard of bisexuals in Indiana. Though you didn't think you'd ever met one, at least not a male one. There had been that girl in college, but you'd never really been sure about her. "You're bi. But you're also taken."

"Fair enough. No harm done, right?" He stands up—"Hey, I think I hear Jamie"—and heads out of your room, through the kitchen, down the hall.

You sit down on the bed again, not sure what to make of what just happened. Michael seemed to take it so lightly—did you make too big a deal out of it? Still, whether or not he's OK with it, whether or not *Jamie* is OK with it—the point is that you aren't OK with it. You don't want to get in between a couple, even a gay couple. If you're going to pick up a guy, you want it to be a guy you can maybe keep for your own someday—with no guilt.

With that thought clear in your mind, you go out to meet Jamie, to chop some onions, to try Vietnamese food. As it turns out, they're closeted in their bedroom—when you pause at their door, you hear sounds that you can't make out. You're tempted to linger, but instead, you turn yourself around and go back into the kitchen. There's a big pile of onions on the counter, and you start peeling. There's also an open bottle of dark liquid—when you sniff it, you feel a little ill.

• PLEASE TURN TO PAGE 53.

Saturday passes in a blur—you do a little shopping, you call your mother, you even work on the genealogy project for a few hours. The software's pretty easy to use; it shouldn't be any trouble to write up. But while maybe a quarter of your brain is focused on the computer, the other three quarters is busy anticipating your date. What will you do? Where will he take you? What does he think of as special? You hope the food isn't too weird . . .

When the buzzer rings, you're ready. You walk quickly down the hall, but Rose beats you to the door—her bedroom's a lot closer. You join her there, and the two of you wait for Peter to climb the stairs. She's just wearing sweatpants and a white T-shirt, but she still looks pretty cute. Really hot, actually, even with all that luxurious hair pulled up in a practical ponytail. Hopefully, Peter won't notice.

When he reaches the top of the stairs, he's looking pretty cute himself—gray sweater, khakis, nothing fancy, but it all looks good on him. You want to slide your hands up under that sweater, under the white T-shirt, and press your hands flat against his skin. Mmm. One hand is tucked behind his back, and as he walks to the door, he pulls it out, flourishing a bouquet of irises, tall stems in deep blues and purples.

"How gorgeous! Thank you," you say.

He hands them to you, smiling. "I thought they'd look good with your eyes, and they do." The words are smooth, but he stammers slightly as he says them. It's charming. You get the feeling that he practiced the lines in his head but wasn't quite ready to say them out loud.

You're blushing at the compliment, but that's OK. Blushes look good on you. "Let me put these in water—I'll just be a minute."

As you walk down the hall, you can hear them talking. Rose says something about sunflowers, but you don't catch the words exactly. Did he bring her flowers when they were dating? Sunflowers would have gone beautifully with her skin. As you put the flowers in a tall vase, you can't help worrying. Does Peter miss her? Does she miss him? You leave the vase on the kitchen table and walk slowly back down the hall, afraid of what you'll see there, but Rose isn't kissing him, and she isn't crying, either. She looks perfectly cheerful and somewhat distracted, like she wants to get back to cleaning the bathroom. When she sees you coming, she gives Peter a quick hug and then turns back down the hall, meeting you and hugging you briefly on the way.

"Have fun, you two. And take a jacket—it's chilly out there!"

And then you're at the door. You grab a jacket, and Peter leads you down the stairs.

It's definitely a bit of a hike. A bus to BART, the train ride across the Bay (under the water!), but the time goes quickly. Peter tells you about himself—he's from Chicago originally, but he's been all over. Undergrad at Princeton, in math, grad school at Chicago, also in math, and now a post-doc at Berkeley, in math, of course. He's in algebraic geometry, whatever that means. It doesn't seem to have much in the way of practical applications, but he says it's a lot of fun. He's hoping Berkeley or Stanford will take him on as a tenure-track professor—that way, he'd get to stay in the Bay Area, which he's fallen in love with.

He talks fast, as if he's nervous. He probably is nervous—it turns out that he hasn't actually dated very much. A few girls here and there, but Rose was his only serious relationship, and that ended years ago. You find that hard to believe—he's *so* cute. But he's also shy; he says that all the girls he's dated asked him out first. You've never dated a math geek before. Maybe they're more fun than football stars. They're certainly less full of themselves.

When you get off the train, you walk a few blocks north and west. You end up at a tiny Italian restaurant, a hole in the wall. Peter leads you inside; the waiter who seats you knows him.

"I come here pretty often. You have to promise me that you won't tell anyone about this place. The food is incredible, and they don't know how much they're undercharging for it."

"I promise—but how did you find it? This is pretty out of the way." You'd taken several turns on narrow streets to get here.

"Well, that's why it's special. I found it a few months after I arrived here." He drinks some water before continuing. You're watching the muscles moving in his smooth throat, and miss the first words of what he says next: ". . . was actually kind of surprised I got this job at Berkeley. My dissertation was fine, but it wasn't outstanding. They told me they thought I had the potential to do something interesting, so they were going to take a chance on me for a year. If I didn't come up with something really good, I was out of here, and I'd probably have ended up teaching at some podunk college in the middle of nowhere."

"Hey, I went to a podunk college!" You're feeling dumb again. You just went to your local college, and you had pretty much a B average straight through. That's not going to impress this guy.

"No offense—it's just that if you're a professor at most schools, you're there to teach, so you teach a lot of classes and you have no time to research. I love research—there are weeks when I don't want to think about anything but math."

Hmm, is that what you want in a boyfriend? Shouldn't he be thinking about you, at least a little every day? Still, it's nice that he likes his job. And it's kind of cool to be dating a professor. When you were in college, you used to fantasize about your Shakespeare professor. He was British and had a hot accent. You used to tune out his lectures, imagining yourself as sexy Desdemona, whose husband thought she was cheating on him but who was really totally in love with him and didn't want anything more than to have sex with him, right there, on that broad classroom desk, and . . . Some of your fantasies didn't make a lot of sense. But even thinking about that one turns you on—your nipples have gotten hard, and you have to concentrate to come back to the here and now, where Peter's still talking: ". . . it's all about time, you know? Time to research, time to teach." He glances down at his empty plate. "Maybe time to have a girlfriend?"

Is he trying to be charming again? Somehow, you don't think his job choice had anything to do with you. Still, the effort is sweet. "Oh, OK. I forgive you for insulting my college. Go on with your story."

Peter nods. "Right. So I'd taken to wandering around Berkeley at night, just walking, thinking, trying to come up with something brilliant. I'd been doing it for months, not having any luck, until finally, one night when I had wandered in here, mostly to get out of the rain, I actually thought of something. Something that might work."

"What?" It's funny, but you do want to know. It's something

about the way he's leaning forward, the way his hand hovers near yours, not quite touching. Something about the passion in his voice—the excitement as he remembers that moment. It's sexy.

"Well, I honestly don't think I can explain it, not unless you want to take a few years of math classes first." The poor boy looks hesitant, like he's afraid of insulting you.

"I'll pass." You don't want to hear a lot of math talk. Instead, you reach out and take his hand in yours. He seems startled but lets you hold it. Before long, he's caressing your hand, absentmindedly. One dark finger reaching out and tracing a ticklish path from your wrist to the tip of your pinkie. Over and over.

"Anyway, suffice it to say, it was good, good enough at least, and Berkeley was pleased and renewed my post-doc for a few more years, and I've been publishing steadily since then, and now it looks like I have a decent shot at that tenure-track job. Which would be amazing."

"And it all happened right here?" You're focused on his hand, on the way the light from the candle shivers over it. Your hand looks strange in his—it's such a sharp contrast. Pale and dark. Startling, but attractive, too.

Peter brings his other hand up to enclose both of yours. Your hands have disappeared into his, and you look up, surprised, to find his eyes intent on your face. "It started here, anyway. That's why this place is special. It seems like a good place to start important things. I've never brought a girl here before. You're the first." His face is utterly serious.

This guy is intense. You're not sure what you think about that. He's clearly headed somewhere serious—is that what you want?

And do you want it with him, a slightly geeky, though very cute, math guy? Or do you want to look for someone else to be serious about, maybe even play the field for while, date around? If you don't want to take him seriously, it would be kinder to end it now, even if you are curious about what he'd be like in bed. If you leave now, you could even get back in plenty of time to go to that sex party with Rose . . .

- *If you decide Peter's just not what you're looking for,* PLEASE TURN TO PAGE 106.

- *If this is going well, and you want to continue,* PLEASE TURN TO PAGE 145.

The hot water feels incredible—they have great water pressure in this apartment. You have it turned up to almost scalding to help get the chill out of your bones. Despite all the walking and the sweating, despite the sunniness of the day, there's still a chill to the air in this city, a dampness that soaks into your skin. It makes you long for a crackling wood fire, the kind your dad would build in the winter. The living room here has a fireplace—maybe you can go get some wood and build a fire this weekend. If the fireplace actually works . . .

For now you'll settle for the pounding hot water, coming down hard on your neck, your shoulders, your back. You could stand here for hours. But you have only half an hour, so you'd better get clean. You reach for the bar of generic soap that you brought in your travel kit, and then reconsider. There's a corner shelf, four levels high, and it's packed with bath supplies. Scrubs and foaming soaps, shampoos with eucalyptus, with mint, with berries. Nut butter, whatever that is. There are pumice stones and sea sponges—you feel like you're in a spa instead of an ordinary shower. Rose did say you could try some of her stuff . . . You shampoo quickly, rinse, rub conditioner through your hair. Then you pick up the cranberry-vanilla scrub and squeeze some out onto a loofah.

You start gently at first, rubbing the loofah up and down your arms. But soon you're rubbing harder, really getting your blood pumping, exfoliating away all those dead cells. You've never bothered much with this kind of thing before, but the scrub feels amazing against your skin—harsh, but not too harsh. Invigorating. You rub the loofah across your shoulders, your stomach, gently over your breasts. Down to your hips and ass, scrubbing harder now.

You raise a leg and balance it against the wall; it's precarious, though, since the wall is slippery and there's no place for a decent hold. You sink down to the floor instead, sitting there with your legs in front of you, scrubbing away all the stress of the last few days. It's been intense.

The shower is filling with a heavenly scent, like Christmas, and you're getting dizzy. But it's a good kind of dizzy, a slight euphoria. You pull your razor off the shelf, shave your armpits quick, then start to work on your very exfoliated legs. Long strokes, from ankle to knee. This you've been doing since you were twelve; you could almost do it in your sleep. You can't remember the last time you cut yourself—it was years ago. The tricky bits are around the ankle and at the knee and along the front bone, the tibia. That's where you have to slow down. But even so, two minutes and you're done with both legs. You slide your hand up and down to check for rough spots but don't find any; you enjoy the silky smoothness of your skin. It feels really good. If you were planning on having sex tonight, you might shave your thighs as well—you might even try shaving a bit more. But sex isn't so likely tonight; even if things go well with Peter, you can't simply take him back to your bedroom. And going back to his place would be a little drastic. So up to the knees will be plenty. Of course, all you have is jeans, so it doesn't matter anyway. You could've skipped shaving entirely. But it feels nice to have your legs so smooth—it feels sexy. It'll be easier to flirt with Peter with shaved legs.

You climb to your feet, a tad unsteadily. It's definitely too hot in here now. You turn the heat down. You're all scrubbed, but you're still not clean, so you pick up some soap. You start with the backs of your ears—if you don't start there, you'll forget to come back to it. Then your neck, your hands moving in slow circles. Your arms, underarms, and then comes the fun. Soaping up your breasts—this is where you always slow down, get distracted. You rub slow circles around your breasts, circling in toward the nipples. You tease yourself a little, coming in, then pulling back, in and back, in and back, until finally your fingers come to rest on your nipples, buried in soapy suds, rubbing lightly across the soft nubs, back and forth until they harden in your palms. You lean against an empty corner, bracing yourself so you don't fall down. You play with your nipples for an endless time, squeezing and rubbing, even pinching, while the muscles in your legs tense and release, until it gets too frustrating. Then you bring your right hand down to your pussy and slide your index finger in; it goes in so easy, so smooth. In as far as you can reach, then out again, sliding up across your clit, really slow, really gentle. You're soaking, and as you slide your finger in and out, as you add a second finger, pushing harder, faster, you can't restrain a moan—it rises up and out of you, and all you can do is hope the water covers the sound. It doesn't matter, though; you don't really care. All you care about now is the water still pounding down on you, getting cooler while you get hotter, your left hand still busy on your breast, your right hand's fingers pumping in and out, deep into your pussy and out again, out against your clit, now rubbing there, rubbing in slow circles, then faster, faster, until you're shoving yourself hard against the shower wall, until your body starts shaking in quick, shuddering spasms, until the waves of pleasure suddenly break over you, and you sink to the shower floor again as the water gets cold.

Before it quite turns to ice water, you manage to pull yourself up, rinse off, find the soap and put it back on the shelf, and climb out. In the hallway, the buzzer rings.

• PLEASE TURN TO PAGE 90.

You take a deep breath, open your door, and walk through. Michael smiles up at you. "Hey."

"Hey." You can't help smiling back at him; he looks like everyone's image of an all-American boy. With more shoulder work, he could be on a football team. He'd probably like that, too. Sweaty locker rooms full of mostly naked men, reaching for the ball between the quarterback's legs—you might like it, too, come to think of it. There were stories back in college of girls who took on the whole football team. What would it be like to try something like that?

But you have something else to think about right now. Jamie's turning in his chair, looking up at you. "Good morning, Kathryn." You can't quite read his tone—a little hesitant, a little friendly. Does he know? He must know. Oh God—he knows that you just had sex with his boyfriend! What the hell are you supposed to do now? What is one supposed to say in this situation? Your mother never taught you the right etiquette for this!

"Good morning, Jamie. How are you?" That's not bad. That's pretty good, actually. You walk over to the counter and pour yourself a cup of coffee. You need coffee. You don't think you can actually eat anything—your stomach's churning a bit. This is so strange.

"Fine, fine. And yourself?" His question is casual, but the tone isn't. It's sort of trembly, actually. You raise your cup to your mouth to give yourself time to think about your answer, watching Michael take a firmer grip on Jamie's hand. Jeez—do you really want to get between these two? Michael's pretty, but is he worth this?

"I'm fine, too." Are you?

"That's good." Jamie stands up then, pulling his hand gently out of Michael's. "I need to get to work. I'll see you guys later." And he walks out of the room and down the hall, leaving his breakfast plate behind. One bite taken out of a piece of perfect toast, the rest untouched.

You hear the front door open and then close heavily. Jamie's gone, leaving you alone with Michael again. You slide into a chair—*not* the one Jamie left. The third chair. Appropriate for you, the third person in this relationship. The third wheel? You're not sure. It's all so confusing.

Michael reaches out and takes your hand in his.

"Hey. You doing OK?" He strokes your hand with his thumb, rubbing the skin gently. It's soothing, comforting. "Sorry to disappear on you, but I wanted to have a chance to tell Jamie about all this before he left for work."

"What did you tell him?" Did he tell Jamie—everything? All the gory details of what you'd been doing in that bedroom?

"I told him that you and I had sex in your bedroom, that I liked it, and that I'd like to do it again, if you're willing."

"And he's OK with that?"

"He's a little nervous. He'd like to meet you for lunch, actually, to talk about it. Will you do that?"

Lunch with Jamie? Your whole plan was to try to ignore Jamie's existence. Lunch doesn't fit into that.

"Do I have to?" You sound pathetic, you know, like a little kid who doesn't want to take her medicine. But you really don't want to take it.

"Jamie's very important to me, Kathryn—I don't want to do

anything that'll hurt him. We push each other's boundaries sometimes, but we don't just slam through them, y'know? So yes, if you want to keep seeing me, I need you to talk to Jamie."

So you're faced with another choice. It seems that all you do in this city is make choices. Is this what the rest of your life will be like, difficult conversations with strange men who have completely different mind-sets from anything you've ever encountered before? It sounds exhausting. Exciting, too, of course—you can still feel the pleasant languor in every inch of your body from the incredible fucking Michael gave you less than an hour ago. But if you keep up this relationship, you have the feeling it's going to be an emotional tightrope, the kind it would be easy to fall off of.

It doesn't seem fair somehow. Why can't you have Michael to yourself? In Indiana, if a girl managed to get someone else's guy to sleep with her, she had at least a decent chance of stealing him away. If Michael enjoyed being with you, maybe he'd consider picking you instead? It couldn't be easy, living a gay lifestyle. He'd blend in so beautifully in Indiana if you brought him home—your mom would love his sweetness, and your girlfriends would go totally nuts over how gorgeous he is.

You could ask, couldn't you? What could it hurt?

Or you could just talk to Jamie the way he wants you to.

• *If you agree to talk to Jamie,* PLEASE TURN TO PAGE 162.

• *If you try to talk Michael into choosing you,* PLEASE TURN TO PAGE 13.

After that, there's not much to say. Peter doesn't want to see you anymore, and you can't really blame him. Sure, he let himself in for it; he gave you tacit permission to do whatever the hell you wanted. But that didn't mean you had to dive straight for the hard-core stuff. You could've paused here and there, checked up on him, made sure that he was doing OK, having fun. You got so caught up in it all, and you ended up going somewhere you never planned to. For a few days, you wallow in guilt and remorse—you never meant to make the boy cry. But it doesn't take long before your common sense reasserts itself—things got out of hand, sure, but no permanent damage was done, and both of you made stupid mistakes that led to all that. It helps that Peter doesn't blame you for it; he blames himself for not being clearer about what he wanted.

Even after you get over the guilt, thinking about Peter makes you sad. But after a few weeks, you're feeling better about it. You'd had a crazy love affair with him, and though it was fun while it lasted, it wasn't based on much of anything real. You both got carried away with all the hot sex, the experimenting, the intensity. You're actually starting to be friends again now; he's not really mad at you about that night. He's just not comfortable having sex with you anymore.

You have to admit that you did enjoy it, though, up until the point where you took off his blindfold and realized that he wasn't enjoying it. It turned you on. Since Peter doesn't want to see you again, you're free to explore other possibilities. Maybe you can find a guy who's into that kind of thing. The San Francisco personals pages have plenty of stuff along those lines. When you talk to Rose about it, she says that she can hook you up with a woman-run dominatrix house, if you want to do it for money. Which you don't think you do, but the idea's intriguing. And apparently there are S&M clubs in the city where you can go in and do whoever looks interesting, assuming they consent. Rose loads you up with a stack of books on S&M stuff—smut, safe sex, safe words, negotiation, how to handle consent issues when your partner is tied up and gagged— these people have worked all this stuff out. No more mistakes like the ones you made with Peter. The next time you get into a relationship, you'll have a much better idea of what you want. Of what turns you on, of what you like doing. You can negotiate all that stuff before you actually do it, so it's a lot less likely to get out of hand. And maybe the next time you meet a cool guy, you'll slow things down a little—that might be a good idea.

It all works out OK in the long run. You still have your great job, they like your work, and they'll probably hire you for another contract gig when this one's done. You get along well with your roommates, even if they are cute enough to be distracting. And you've really adapted to San Francisco life—you've turned into the kind of girl that your Midwest friends wouldn't recognize. And you know what? You like it. You are going to have yourself a really good time.

THE END

I'll take that risk—there are risks with any relationship, right? What's the divorce rate at these days, anyway?" Not that you actually know anyone who's divorced. In Greendale, people stay in their marriages, miserable or not.

"Pretty damn high," he says, smiling.

"Let's live dangerously." You smile back at him, and then both of you stand up. The pieces of napkin are still around your feet, mute testament to how stressful all this might get. But that doesn't mean it's not worth trying. "Is tomorrow a good day for antiquing?"

"Tomorrow's perfect," Jamie says.

"Great! I have to get back for a job interview now, but I'll see you at dinner tonight, OK?"

"Sure." He leans forward and gives you a quick hug, and then you walk off in opposite directions. Life's getting very interesting. . . .

• PLEASE TURN TO PAGE 225.

You can do this. Just slow it down. It's not about the stripping, anyway—it's about the dancing, about the men's eyes on you, enjoying you, feasting on your curves, so hungry for you that they're willing to keep putting quarters in a little machine just to be able to look at your almost naked body through glass.

You keep sliding your hands along your body, moving gently to the music. All around the room, the windows keep sliding open and closed again. Some men have clearly laid claim to their booths tonight, checking out the new girls. Some men come for a few minutes, then come, then leave. You are glad that you can see only their faces, that there is no ledge for them to stand on, no way for them to press their penises into your face. You aren't ready for that, not yet. Just faces, dimly seen through the glass.

You caress your breast—in front of people, something you'd never done even in front of John. It's exciting, and you never would have done it in Indiana. In Greendale, Kathryn was a girl who let her fiancé touch her, a little. If she touched herself, she did so in private, when it was very late and her door was locked. Here, you can touch yourself in a roomful of women, some of whom are looking at you occasionally, checking out the competition. You can lick your lips the way a porn star might, you can slide your fingers across your waist, into the waistband of your red panties, across the blond curls that the men can see only the edges of. You can dip a finger inside yourself, then bring your finger up, slowly, and taste the salty musk of it. You're getting wet from the dancing and the music, from the eyes on you and your own hands on your skin. No one's ever lusted after you like this. And it's not just one man—there might be as many as a dozen here, watching you slip a bra strap down, then another, letting your breasts move more freely. You run a finger across your right nipple, which hardens in your hand. It's chilly here, encouraging your nipples to harden, your body to move. It feels really good to move.

That same girl, a curvy dark-skinned girl, perhaps from India, leans over again. "Better, but remember—this is all a tease. You get a flat rate for working this room; what you want to do is hook a guy and get him to pay for a private show."

"There's still glass between us, right?" You're talking and moving at the same time. It's not quite dancing, but it's close enough for the men.

"Right, but he gets to sit down, and there's a two-way intercom; it's almost like being together. That's what they tell themselves, anyway. You can do more in there, too—we're not supposed to do penetration out here, for example."

She's moving the whole time she's whispering to you, slow shimmies of large hips and thighs. She's not a small woman, but she's very sexy still.

"Thanks for filling me in."

"No problem. Hey, looks like they're done with us. Now we get to see who made the cut."

The windows all close, and a door opens. An older woman starts herding you out. In the hallway, she divides you into two groups— one large, one small. You're in the smaller group, along with the Indian girl. You've made the cut. Now comes the interesting part: the private room.

• PLEASE TURN TO PAGE 5.

Y ou bring your finger back up to your lips and lick it clean. You like this game.

But the paddle's clearly not good enough. You switch toys: now it's the short whip, one with many strands. There's a different name for this kind of whip, you remember from the toy store—a cat-o'-nine-tails. You hit him lightly with it once, just to get the feel for it. It hits very softly. It doesn't seem like much of an S&M toy at all, to be honest. But if you remember the stories right, it's one of those where you have to build up to it—if you keep hitting him with it, over and over in the same places, it's going to get very sensitive there, it's going to hurt. Of course, that's going to take a lot of hitting. Your arm might get tired; it's not like you've exercised it much with this kind of activity. Maybe you'd be better off going directly for the good stuff. You drop the cat and pick up the riding crop.

Now, *this* is a toy. Hell, it's practically a weapon. You bring it down quickly onto his butt, and this time Peter practically jumps off the bed—ooh, that baby's gotta sting! He yelps, too, and then mumbles something through the gag. You could take it off, but you aren't interested in hearing what he has to say, are you? If you were, you would have asked him before you started playing. Now you're turned on, you're enjoying this, and he'd better shut up and take it. He asked for it, didn't he?

You bring the crop down again and again, in a new place each time so he can't anticipate and brace for it. His ass. The crease where ass meets thigh. His shoulders. His calves. The small of his back. But mostly his ass—over and over you come back to his ass. It's so luscious, and every time you hit it, he jumps. He stops yelping after a while, but he can't stop jumping. You hit him with the crop until your arm really does get tired, until thin welts crisscross his back. You didn't actually break the skin, but it's kind of impressive. Sexy somehow, to see him marked up like that. It makes you really hot, and you don't want to wait anymore for your own satisfaction. You roll him over again—he doesn't fight you, but he isn't helping, either. His cock's only half hard, but a spit and a few quick strokes fix that. Then you're straddling him, sliding onto him, bouncing on the bed and fucking him hard, and it's not long before you're coming, coming hard and digging your nails into his chest while you do it. You collapse onto him, exhausted.

It's only then that you remove the blindfold. Only then that you notice the marks of tears on the fabric. Only then that you remove the gag and hear Peter saying softly, repeatedly, "Please, please stop." Only then that you realize this has gone much too far.

• PLEASE TURN TO PAGE 128.

You don't need this. You pull on the black gown, head down to the dressing room, and throw on your street clothes as quickly as you can. You feel sick, and you desperately want a shower. The man's words keep echoing in your head.

You don't look for Rose; you leave the club without speaking to anyone and go straight back to the apartment. You undress and climb into the shower, turning the water as hot as it will go. It's scalding your skin and you're scrubbing hard, but you still don't feel clean. You don't think you'll ever feel clean, not as long as you're in this city. The guys in Greendale might have been boring, but they were never as bad as that man. You climb out, dry off, dress in several layers of clothing, covering yourself from neck to wrists to toes. You pack your bags and write a note to the roommates, telling them you're sorry, this isn't going to work, that they should send what remains of your rent and deposit money to your mother's address. And then you're gone, out the door, down to the Greyhound station, buying a ticket for home.

Your pulse doesn't calm down until you're an hour away from San Francisco. You can't even process it all yet—you don't know if you're glad you came to the city or not. Right now all you're doing is counting the hours until you're home again, home in your mother's house, in your own sheltering bed. Maybe you'll call John again someday. At the moment, you don't want to think about men, about sex. All you want is to be safe at home again. You'll be there soon. It'll all be OK. Just a little while longer . . .

THE END

You decide to go for it—to push Peter a little, see what happens. You slide your hand up his thigh, onto his cock. He tenses up; you can feel the muscles tighten in the arm across your shoulders. You move your other hand down, unbuttoning your jeans. You unzip your jeans. They're loose enough that you don't even have to push them down; you can just fit your hand inside, far enough to slide under the blue panties, over your soft golden fur, down to where your clit nestles, wet and hard, aching. You don't have much freedom of movement, but you can move your finger back and forth, back and forth. Peter's frozen, looking past you, out the window. He isn't participating at all, but his cock is rock-hard under your hand. He's definitely turned on. You're getting close, but you don't want to come alone. You want him to share this with you. So you move your hand on his cock, start sliding it up and down, caressing it—and that's when he stops you.

"No."

That's it. Just the one word and he's pulling away, standing up, leaving you alone in your seat with your hand still stuck in your pussy, your finger stopping just short of bringing you off. You could scream, but then everyone in the train car would be looking at you both. You're surprised they aren't already.

"I can't do this, Kathryn. I'm sorry. I really liked you." He says the words softly, just loud enough for you to hear. He waits for a minute, as if to see whether you're going to apologize, try to get him back. But you don't need this kind of shit. If you wanted some boring old prude, you'd have stuck with John. Jesus Christ! You deliberately look away, out the train window. Peter walks away, crossing into another car. You masturbate until you come, but it isn't much good. It's going to be a long ride home.

• PLEASE TURN TO PAGE 22.

What you actually see when you open the door a crack and peer through is even worse, somehow. Jamie, quietly dressed in a sharply tailored suit, frying two eggs. He deftly flips them and then slides them out onto two plates, one egg each. Two pieces of toast pop up, and he adds those to the plates. Slices of honeydew. He lays the plates down on the table, where two large glasses of orange juice are already waiting, and slides into the chair that faces away from your door just as Michael comes out of the shower, one towel wrapped around his waist, another rubbing his wet blond hair. Michael bends down and kisses the top of Jamie's head. "Thanks, sweetie." He slides into the other chair and starts to eat.

It's all so sweet, so domestic. They're a nice couple, from what you've seen. And maybe Jamie will be OK with all this, but maybe he won't. You could ask him. It would be awkward, incredibly awkward. Maybe he'll hate you for this. You're not sure how you feel about them, seeing them together. There are definitely some twinges of something in the vicinity of your chest. It's not like you're in love with Michael or anything. But you've just shared something very intimate, something you've shared with only one other person before. And there he is, having breakfast with his boyfriend, and here you are, alone. This all feels very strange.

You could talk to Jamie about it, or you could try to ignore him and keep seeing Michael on the side. Maybe it would be OK. Maybe you'll get used to seeing them together. It's all in your hands right now.

Jamie reaches out a hand and Michael takes it in his, lacing their fingers together. They keep eating, not saying a word.

- *If you decide to talk to Jamie about all this,* PLEASE TURN TO PAGE 234.

- *If you want to pretend that Jamie doesn't exist,* PLEASE TURN TO PAGE 125.

He does look like he's slept in his clothes. Normally immaculate, John is rumpled and exhausted. His eyes have dark circles under them; his forehead has more lines than you remember. You can't stop staring at him—despite everything, he looks good. He still looks like the football star you fell in love with oh so many years ago. Maybe it's nostalgia that makes him look so good. When you look at him, you don't see just him. You see your mother, your cousins. Your house in Indiana, with two full stories, plus an attic, plus a finished basement. Not to mention the root cellar. Your mom's tuna-noodle casserole, baked with potato chips on top. Jell-O salad. Snow blanketing the roofs, lying heavy on the bare branches of trees. Roaring fires. You look at him, and you see home.

"Katie, say something. Say something, please."

It's that edge of desperation in his voice that knocks you out of it, brings you back to here, San Francisco, your apartment. Your roommates are all home, but they've disappeared into their rooms, giving you what privacy they can.

"Hi, John." You can't help it then—you step forward and slide into his arms, just for a moment. They close around you, tentatively at first, then harder, finally squeezing you so hard that again, you can barely breathe. He feels so different from Peter. He feels good. "I missed you, too."

And it's true, you did, though you didn't realize it until now. Solid, boring John—but he's not so boring now, is he? He did something completely random, completely unlike him. If he's changed enough to do that, how much else has he changed? How much else *can* he change, especially if you help? You've learned a lot in San Francisco—you could go back to Greendale and try to educate John.

Sex toys and ice cubes, candle wax and feathers, photos and videos—you could go back to Greendale and try to educate John. And John doesn't have Peter's hang-up about public sex; when you stop and think about it, there was plenty of making out in public back in Indiana, at the movie theater, at the lake, in the woods near John's parents' house. Maybe you could get John to go even further than Peter was willing to. John *is* head over heels in love with you, after all—that might be a powerful motivator. And maybe you're still more than a little in love with him. Sweet John. Did you give up too easily on him?

"I know you think I'm boring, Katie, but I can change. I can do whatever you want, I can be different. Just give me a chance—we can make it work. I swear." He's whispering the words against your hair, still holding you tight, like he'll never let you go. "Just come back with me."

It's up to you. Do you want to give John another chance? San Francisco hasn't brought you true love, not yet. You might never find it here. You have work, you have roommates, you date—is that enough for you? Maybe the real question isn't where you'll have the best sex, but where you'd be most at home. Could Greendale handle the new Kathryn? Maybe it always could, but you only needed to go away for a bit to find her.

• *If you want to try again with John,* PLEASE TURN TO PAGE 204.

• *If you want to stay in San Francisco and send John home,* PLEASE TURN TO PAGE 177.

You wake up to a shaft of bright sunlight through your window—Friday morning, your second morning in the city. When you stumble out into the kitchen, Michael's sitting at the dining table, a cup of coffee in front of him, steam still rising from a pot on the counter.

You smile happily. "Oh, good—I was starting to think the only thing people drank in this house was hot chocolate." You fish a clean mug out of the dish rack, pour yourself some coffee, gulp it down, a little shocked by the way it scalds your throat, by the harsh bitterness of it. You'd been a cream-and-two-sugars girl back in Indiana, but after visiting a peep show last night, maybe you should turn into a black-coffee girl. You forgot to call your mom the other day, to tell her you'd arrived safely. You've been in the city only two days, and already you're changing.

Michael grins, his bright blue eyes sparkling. "Well, actually, I put some cocoa and two sugars in my coffee. I like it sweet. But you can have it straight up, if you want."

Straight up. You'd like him straight up. He's not wearing a shirt again, and the angle of the table is blocking your view from waist to thighs. He could just as well be naked. The morning sun is streaming down, bathing him in light. His body is massive and very delectable—and also, you remind yourself again, very taken. Some girls might go after a guy like that; some girls wouldn't.

• *If you might go after a guy like that,* PLEASE TURN TO PAGE 65.

• *If you're the sort to leave Michael to his boyfriend,* PLEASE TURN TO PAGE 58.

"Come on, Michael—you can't really mean that." You lean forward, slide your hands up his arms, coming to rest on his broad chest. Moving quickly, you slip out of your chair to end up kneeling at his feet. You grab the white towel and pull it away from his crotch, baring the gorgeous cock that was pounding into you so recently. You bend down and put your mouth on it, sucking it in as fast as you can, not wanting to think about what you're doing. You've never done this before, but you've heard that it drives men crazy, that they can't think when a woman's sucking their cock. The porn Web sites you've stumbled across are full of photos of men coming all over a woman's face, presumably right after she sucks him off. You suck hard, wanting to get it over with—you're not turned on right now, but you know what you want. You want Michael, and you want him to be all yours. If this is what it takes to get him . . .

"Jesus!" And his hands are on your head, pushing you off him. "What the hell do you think you're doing?"

"I thought you'd like it."

"First, I didn't invite you to do that. Second, if I had, you knew that the condition was that you talk to Jamie first, which you clearly aren't willing to do."

"But—"

"And third, that was the worst thing my cock has ever experienced. If you want to learn how to suck cock, girl, you shouldn't start on a gay man. Find a nice inexperienced straight boy who won't care if you suck like a vacuum cleaner. Ow!"

"I'm—I'm sorry."

"This is not going to work. You don't have any understanding of boundaries—there's no way I can trust you not to hurt Jamie. Hell, I don't trust you not to hurt me! I'm going to talk to Rose right now. I hate to wake her up, but I think she'll agree that given all this, you're not a good match for us. You're going to have to find a new place to live, and some new guy to assault."

"I thought you would like it."

"You can come back when you've learned to ask first!"

And he's gone, knocking on Rose's door, disappearing into her room.

• PLEASE TURN TO PAGE 38.

"Hey, that's really sweet." You squeeze his hands gently. Peter smiles, looking relieved. The waiter comes by and pours some wine. You're not sure you're going to need any—it's intoxicating just having a guy be so into you, and so up-front about it. Even when you were engaged, John never trusted you this much; he was never so emotionally naked.

The rest of dinner is less intense but no less pleasurable. You enjoy Peter's conversation, even laugh at a few of his math jokes, though you're not quite sure you get them. When it ends, Peter escorts you back across the Bay, up to the apartment. He walks you to the top of the stairs, and you suddenly feel awkward—you're not sure if you want to invite him in, but even if you wanted to, you'd promised Rose you wouldn't. But he doesn't ask if he can come in, he just leans forward and kisses you. And again, it's dizzying; your lips lock together and electricity is sizzling through you. Your hands lace behind his back, pulling him against you. His fingers are moving on your neck, your shoulders, pushing aside your jacket to linger against naked skin. Peter's mouth opens and his tongue touches yours—you moan, and it's just too much. You reach behind you, fumble with the door. You manage to swing it open, but before you can pull Peter inside, he's breaking the kiss, pulling back.

"I'll call you?" He's breathing hard. He doesn't look like he wants to stop.

"Um, sure. OK." You definitely don't want to stop. But now that he's not actually kissing you, you can think more clearly. This wouldn't be a good idea, bringing him inside.

"OK." Peter bites his bottom lip, looking suddenly uncertain. Then he takes a quick breath, turns, and clatters down the stairs. This time, he doesn't trip.

• PLEASE TURN TO PAGE 175.

You jerk away from Michael, pulling your tank down to cover your chest before you even make sense of the words, curling in on yourself since there's nothing you can do about the lost jeans. A slender man leans on the doorway to your room. Dark auburn hair, pale skin, a well-cut gray suit.

"Hello, Jamie-love. Home safe and sound . . ." Michael says, still lying on the bed. You scooch back against the wall, pulling the sheet up to cover you, up to your chest, moving as far away from Michael as you can, which is not that far at all, even on such a big bed.

"And right on time, as usual," Jamie says. "So, were you planning on inviting me to your little party? Or did you just pick this one up for your own fun?"

"This isn't what it looks like, love." Michael still sprawls on the bed—even his long body is dwarfed by its size. What are you going to do with a bed this big? All your stuffed elephants from home wouldn't be enough to fill it.

"No?" You can't read anything in Jamie's tone. Is he upset? Is he angry at Michael? At you? What the hell just happened?

"This is our new roommate, Jamie. Meet Miss Kathryn." Michael's finally sitting up, sweeping an arm in your direction, like a noble at court.

"Ah, Kathryn. Nice to meet you." Jamie nods coolly in your direction. "I'm James, as you've probably figured out. And now I'd like to talk to my boyfriend in our bedroom, if you'll excuse us?"

You nod, not sure what else to do. When you were in second grade, you kissed Betsy Caldwell's boyfriend's cheek, but this doesn't seem quite the same. Betsy hadn't minded, in any case. She already had a new boyfriend—she just hadn't told her old one yet. Definitely not the same.

Jamie turns and walks away; Michael gives you an apologetic shrug and follows after him. You don't know if you should lie down on your bed and cry or go into the kitchen and chop onions. At least there you'd have an excuse for crying.

In the end, you get up and get your bag. You unpack it quickly and finally finish drying off—with your door securely closed and locked. You change into clean jeans and a long-sleeve shirt, buttoned all the way up. Dry socks. Shoes. Does Jamie think you're a slut? Are you a slut? Was that sex? You barely touched Michael, but God—the things he did to you, it sure felt like sex. Like the best sex you've ever had.

They're still closeted in their bedroom. For lack of anything else to do, you go into the kitchen.

You peel four onions, then another. They're still in the bedroom. You chop the onions automatically, the way you would for your mother's spaghetti sauce. When you're finished, you stare at them, not sure if that was the right thing to do. Maybe Jamie wanted them sliced, or minced. Too late now.

Eventually, they come out of the bedroom. Jamie doesn't seem to mind the chopped onions; he takes over the cooking, shooing you over to sit down at the table with Michael. He peels ginger, grates it, cleans bean sprouts and tosses them in the pot along with cinnamon and other spices you can't name. He pulls a package of chicken thighs out of the fridge and cleans off the fat, skimming over the skin with a sharp knife. You can't seem to take your eyes off the knife. If it were you catching your boyfriend with somebody else, you'd be feeling some violent urges. But Jamie's so calm, so collected. It's as if nothing has happened at all. You have no idea how he feels.

You stay at the table, politely, though you want to run. When the meal is over, you make your excuses and go straight to bed. You dream of Michael—his hands, his golden body, making love to you. You're both naked, rolling around on the covers. And Jamie's there, too, sitting cross-legged on the bed in a full business suit, silent, watching.

You wake up in a cold sweat to the sound of loud knocking on your door. You're certain it's Jamie, finally coming to give you what you deserve for messing with his boyfriend. Your throat is tight, and you can't bring yourself to call out and invite him in. The door opens anyway, without waiting for your call.

It isn't Jamie.

• PLEASE TURN TO PAGE 55.

Y ou sigh, but you let your hand drop from your breast and remove your other hand from his thigh. It's the right thing to do, even if it sucks.

"It would've been fun." You can still imagine what it would have been like—unbuttoning your jeans and sliding your hand down, inside your panties, to find your hard, wet clit—your poor body is thrumming with desire.

"Not for me, I'm afraid." Peter takes your hands in his, squeezes them. He kisses your forehead gently. "Thank you for stopping."

"All you have to do is ask." And even though it's difficult, you do mean that—you like this guy, and if this is going to work at all, you figure he has to be able to trust you. Pushing a little is OK, but no means no. Some of the guys in high school had trouble with that concept; you don't plan on turning into someone like that. You take a deep breath and lean against him again. The train ride will be over soon. You'll count the minutes until then.

That's when Peter wraps his arm around your shoulders, leans over, and starts whispering in your ear. Very softly. You can barely hear him, but what he's saying makes you shiver. Whispering that he wants you so much that he can barely think straight. That you drive him crazy. That you smell incredible, and that he wants to lick you all over. He wants to touch every inch of your skin, wants to kiss your breasts, your hips, your thighs. He wants to suck your toes. You clasp your hands together to keep from touching him again. You close your eyes and listen to his whispering until you feel like you're going to explode, and then you whisper, "You know, this isn't helping." He whispers back, "I know." And then he keeps going, telling you how he wants to lick you, first slow and soft, then quick and hard.

It's very dark behind your closed eyes; it's a long, long ride to the Berkeley station.

The walk to his apartment passes in a blur. Once you're inside, you unbutton his shirt and pull it off. You take off his belt. You walk backward into a room with a bed and unbutton his pants, unzip them and tug them down. He's already stepping out of his shoes, pulling off your T-shirt, unzipping your jeans. He needs both hands to pull them down—you help, surprised at how impatient you feel. It's not just that you're horny, though you are. You feel like you've been waiting to have sex with this man for weeks, months, even though you met him only a few days ago. You can't explain it, but there it is. There'll be time later to take it slow—right now you want him inside you as quickly as possible.

He's wearing tight cotton boxers, black. You have just enough time to notice them before you're pulling them off, falling back onto the bed with only your bra and panties left. He pauses for a moment to look at you, to smile appreciatively. Then he unhooks your bra, pulling it off your shoulders. He hesitates then—and you pull your panties off yourself, impatiently. He starts caressing your breasts again, and it's very lovely, very nice, but just not what you need right now. You can feel his cock, naked and hard against your thigh, and that's what you want. But he doesn't seem to get it—he's starting to lick your nipple again. You're going to have to ask for what you want. Quick breath, and then get the words out, before you have time to think.

"Peter—would you fuck me now? Please?" You reach into your discarded jeans pocket and pull out the condom, offer it to him.

He looks bewildered for a second, but then he goes for it. He tears the wrapper open, slides the condom on in a quick motion, and lowers himself onto you, spreading your legs wide and sliding into you. No more foreplay necessary—you've been wet since the park and even wetter since the train, and you take him easily. He's just the right thickness, just enough so you can feel every inch of him sliding up inside you—and he's long! Long enough that he has to be careful when he gets all the way in; he's pushed right up against your cervix. John always fell short, poor boy.

But you're not thinking about John anymore; you're thinking about Peter, sweet, glorious Peter who's fucking you, sliding in and out in smooth motions that are already sending you up and up, making you dizzy. You reach to meet him, your hips arching, your breasts sliding against his smooth chest, your arms locked around his neck. Back and forth, in and out until you're both sweaty and slippery, and you're *still* going up and up with no end in sight and it's driving you crazy; you can't take much more of this. Finally you give up and shove him again so that he rolls over, and now you're on top. You're on top and you can ride him now, you can slide your clit over his pubic bone, wet and slippery and yes, that is exactly what you needed, to have his cock thick and deep inside you and your clit rubbing up against him, that's what you need to send you up and up and finally over the damned top, until you come in a shiny explosion of sparks, until you come screaming into the light.

Somewhere in there he comes, too, which is nice.

→

Afterward, you do it again. And again. There's some talking, too, and at some point very late at night, when he's fallen asleep with his head on your stomach, you realize that you could really like this guy. Oh, you don't think you're in love with him or anything. You did meet him less than a week ago. But he's got a lot going for him—he's sweet, and earnest, and passionate. And he's great in bed. Maybe not tremendously technically skilled; he doesn't have a big repertoire of sex tricks or anything like that. But he pays attention to your body, to your responses, to everything you say or do. He's patient when you need him to be patient, and he's eager the rest of the time. He wants you, and it feels incredible.

The next few weeks are very interesting. Peter's willing to try almost anything you suggest. Feathers. Candle wax. Ice cubes. The ice cubes are particularly good. It's maybe a week after your day in the park. You call first, asking him to have some ice cubes ready. You tell him what you want him to do with them. He says they'll be ready when you arrive.

You meet Peter on campus, picking him up outside of class. One of the students, a cute little redhead, tries to keep him talking, but he brushes her off with a comment that she should e-mail him with any other questions. Then he takes your hand, striding across campus so quickly that you have to hurry to keep up. He's talking about math again—some paper that he was working on with a colleague in England. You let it wash over you; you can tell by how quickly he's talking that he isn't paying attention to his words, either, he's simply filling his nervousness with words. When you get back to his apartment, you slowly strip for him, pulling off your shirt, peeling off your jeans. You lie down on the bed, still in bra and panties. It's his job to get the bowl of ice from the fridge, to trace lines of ice along your skin, following the path of bones. To follow the wet trail of water with little kisses. To unclasp your bra and slide it off, to circle an ice cube around your breast, spiraling it up slowly until it finally hits the firm peak of your nipple. He plays with you, holding the ice cube there until you're first numb, then almost in pain—then he pulls it away and dives down with his wet, hot, eager mouth, sucking your nipple fiercely into his mouth, making you arch up with the sharp incredible pleasure of it, the sudden rush racing through you, blinding you with its intensity. And then he does it again, and again. The other nipple. Then down, down to your clit, and this is almost too much but you urge him on, you want more, more, more. And he pushes ice cubes inside you, pulls them out again, back and forth until you are begging for his cock, for something long and hard that won't melt away inside you. And then he fucks you silly.

Once he really *gets* the idea of experimenting, he starts coming up with new ideas himself. Sex toys—he takes you to Good Vibrations and buys you a vibrator, then watches while you use it. You get a dildo, a little thicker than him but not quite as long. He ties you up with his ties and teases you for hours without letting you come. He says the alphabet against your clit, counts to a hundred, a thousand, counts in Russian, in French. It drives you crazy. Over a few weeks of spending every night at his place, you manage to work through quite a few positions of the Kama Sutra. You find riding on top of him the most sexually satisfying, but there's something inescapably romantic about good old missionary position, kissing while he pumps into you, gazing into each other's eyes.

• PLEASE TURN TO PAGE 56.

Hey, can we move this into the bedroom? I'd hate for one of the others to walk in on us." Your voice sounds breathy, but at least you managed to get the words out.

"Sure." Michael's response is easygoing, but you catch a flicker of disappointment on his face. Guess you're not quite as exciting as he hoped you'd be. Well, maybe you can show him something exciting once you get to the bedroom.

You stand up on slightly wobbly legs and lead the way to your bedroom. You can feel him slightly behind you. He closes the door behind him, and you can't help it, you have to ask. "Lock it, please?" You're not wild enough to risk Jamie coming looking for his boyfriend and finding you there. Michael clicks the lock shut, and you relax.

"So, what do you want—" Before you can finish the question, he's answering it, stepping close and pushing you gently back on the bed. He catches you before you fall all the way back, holding you up just long enough to pull your flannel shirt up over your head, leaving you bare from the waist up. He pushes you down, and his hands slide along your body, from collarbone to breasts to waist, and then they're pulling off your pants, too, and you're naked. He kneels at the foot of your bed, his hands pushing your legs apart just enough for his mouth to find your pussy, his tongue to lick quickly across your clit. It's all happening so fast, faster than you can keep up with. But maybe you don't have to keep up with it; maybe you just have to lie back and enjoy the incredible sharp sensation of his tongue darting across your clit, quick bright licks that turn slow and soft. Michael's entire mouth is moving on you, and you lose track of what exactly he's doing—it doesn't seem to matter. It all feels so good.

But you want more, and your hands are on him now, urging him up. You want him inside you. Your toes have stroked his cock, and you know exactly how long and thick it is. John had nothing to compare. You want to know what it's like to have something like that inside you, stretching you, filling you up. You're not even sure if you can take it all, but you want to try. Michael moves up obediently, his chest against your breasts, his mouth descending to kiss yours. You can taste yourself on his wet lips, a damp muskiness that doesn't taste good exactly, but it tastes like sex. It tastes hot. It makes you want to fuck him even more, and you arch your pelvis, trying to reach him.

"Hey, hey. That's not going to work. Not safe, Katie-girl. Give me a minute." And he's rolling away, unlocking the door, slipping out. His words a splash of icy water right in your face. Shit. Of course it's not safe to fuck a bisexual man in San Francisco without a condom—it's not safe to fuck any man without a condom unless you're monogamous and preferably married and what the hell were you thinking? You weren't thinking—is it this guy who drives you so crazy that you lose the brains God gave you, or is it you? You're shivering. Is this wild sex, the kind Sally told you about? Or is it just stupidity?

• *If you want to call the whole thing off,* PLEASE TURN TO PAGE 3.

• *If you want to keep going,* PLEASE TURN TO PAGE 75.

"Yes," you say, very softly. His thumb slides up again, briefly, long enough to plunge into your pussy and emerge covered with slick juice. It travels down again, presses against your ass, slow but insistent, pressing in tiny pulses, entering a little farther each time, and the sensation is indescribable, it's like nothing you've felt before. It makes your eyes squeeze shut, hard, and your pussy clench around his other fingers, and it's not long before it's in all the way, and the last finger in your pussy, too, his entire hand shoved up inside you, pumping slowly in and out, pulling you toward him and pushing you away, and you feel like you're about to scream, but you can't get there, not quite yet …

"I'd like to fuck you there," Michael says, his mouth so close that you can feel his breath against your skin. "I'd like to take you right now, push you up against the wall and fuck you up the ass, for a long time. Can I do that?"

You have never imagined letting anyone do that to you before—you hadn't understood why he might even want to, but now, now you don't care why he wants to, all you know is that you want more, more than this thumb shivering through you. You want to be fucked up the ass until you scream. So you say, "Yes."

Michael smiles—you can't see it with your eyes closed, but you can tell. And then he pulls his thumb and fingers out of you, sending a shiver through you. He stands up and walks slowly, naked, around the table. He pulls you up, pushes the chair back and out of the way, and spins you around so you're pressed up against the wall with its peeling yellow wallpaper. His hands are busy on your ass, spreading your cheeks wide, squeezing them hard. His cock's already shoving against your asshole, pushing in.

You don't know what you'd expected—you hadn't thought it would be so hard, so fast. But it feels good. His mouth comes down to chew on the soft flesh of your shoulder; his cock pushes farther in, the weight of his body shoving you hard against the wall. It hurts, a sharp piercing pain, but his hand has come down, his fingers are busy on your clit, and his other hand comes up to squeeze your breast hard, to pinch your nipple, and everything hurts and everything feels good, feels great, all at once. You can't think, you can't tell the sensations apart—it's all sensation, all intense. And now he's biting down harder, he's shoving farther in, tearing you open, farther and farther in until he's there, he's all the way, buried to the hilt inside you. And then he starts to move.

Oh, God. You may never have normal sex again. This is so much stronger, so much fiercer. The first few strokes hurt, but then all the pain disappears. It's sheer pleasure now, a deep, moaning pleasure that has you clawing at the wall as if you're going to climb right through it, has you shoving back against him with each thrust of his cock into your ass, shoving hard, to get him as deep inside you as he can possibly be. You slow for a while, savoring every inch sliding into you, then you start going faster again. The pleasure's growing, incredibly, and you want more. Faster and harder, pounding against him, against the wall, until your entire body is thrumming, and you're groaning out loud now, you're shivering and shaking, you're losing yourself entirely. You're coming again, and again, and again. You're not you, you're just a body, a body being fucked in the ass, and he's biting your shoulder, squeezing both breasts now, slamming you up against the wall faster and faster until finally, finally he comes, collapsing exhausted against you, still buried in your ass.

After a long moment, he pulls out. You open your eyes to the sound of clapping.

→

J amie's there in the doorway, clapping languidly. His face is entirely calm, but his eyes look oddly wounded nonetheless. You hadn't known that you could see pain in a person's eyes like that.

He's not the problem, though.

Rose is there, too, in the doorway, and she's not clapping. You can't name the mixture of emotions crossing her face—is that anger? Disgust? Exasperation? Maybe some of each. You grab your pajama pants and pull them on, but it's a little late for all of that. Rose has started talking, fast and furious.

"Listen, we all like sex. And we all like sex with Michael. He's good at it. But sex with Michael in the kitchen, without checking with us first—well, that's just not cool. You know?"

You nod, not sure what to say. Before you can say anything, she goes on.

"I haven't deposited your rent check yet. I'll give it back to you; I think you should find another place to live."

Just like that? That isn't fair! But she turns and is gone. Jamie stands there a minute longer, looking not at you but at Michael. When he finally speaks, he's not talking to you.

"In the kitchen? Tacky, Michael. Very tacky."

"Hey, Jamie. Sweetheart." Michael's up and out of the chair, not bothering with the towel, and nakedly following his boyfriend down the hallway to their bedroom.

• PLEASE TURN TO PAGE 38.

"Well, I wouldn't want to hurt Jamie . . ."

Michael beams. "Great! He wants to have lunch with you today, to talk all this over. OK?"

"Um, OK." What did you just agree to? And is it too late to back out?

• PLEASE TURN TO PAGE 39.

Y ou touch his hand, gently, interrupting the flow of words. "Jamie, I'm sorry, but I don't feel that way about you. If this means that you don't want me to see Michael, I'll understand."

"No, no. It's OK. Look, I wasn't saying I was in love with you or anything, only that I found you attractive. That doesn't happen to me so often with women, so it seemed worth saying. But it's fine if you don't feel the same way—probably better. I've never spent more than a night with a woman; I don't even know if I could sustain interest in one over time."

You don't know whether to be flattered or insulted. Safer to be neither, to try to be as calm and friendly as possible. "So, where are we now?"

"Well, if you're still interested in dating Michael, I'd like us to be friends. Maybe we could go antiquing sometime? You might enjoy that. And I'll loan you a copy of this book, *The Ethical Slut*— it's a pretty good guide on how to navigate this kind of multiperson relationship. It's not exactly a how-to book, though there's some of that; it's mostly people telling their own stories, what worked for them, what didn't. There are tips on managing jealousy, negotiating, that kind of thing. Some of our friends are in nontraditional relationships of one sort or another—it seems to take an awful lot of talking, but some of them do make it work. Of course, some of them go up in flames, too. There's always a risk."

Do you want to take that risk? It sounds like this could get awfully complicated, and when you got into it, all you really wanted was some fun sex. You could probably get that elsewhere, without risking your relationship with your roommates—or their

relationship with each other. The ball's back in your court now—
what do you want to do with it?

• *If you decide to bow out of the whole thing,* PLEASE TURN TO PAGE 46.

• *If you decide to go for it,* PLEASE TURN TO PAGE 130.

You release his hands and sit back in your chair. "This isn't for me, Michael. I'm sorry. Why don't you tell me about that job interview?"

Michael looks a little disappointed, but maybe also a little relieved. You're not sure, and now you'll probably never know. He starts telling you about the job, which sounds fine, but you're not taking much in. Once you get the details from him—where to go, what to wear—you give him a brief hug and go back to your room. Time to hide under the covers for a while and think about what might have been.

Maybe you'll call your mother. She probably misses you.

• PLEASE TURN TO PAGE 61.

"I don't think I can do this, Rose." You apologize to her, feeling obscurely guilty for disappointing her. She had gone to all this trouble.

Rose shrugs. "Well, hey, stripping isn't for everyone. It's good to know your own boundaries. But listen, I start my shift soon. Can you get yourself home OK? It's a bit of a hike from here to there, but I can tell you what bus to take."

"That'd be fine, thanks. I'm really sorry about this." You pull on your shirt again.

"No worries, chica." She gives you a hug. "I'll see you in the morning."

You finish dressing quickly and find yourself relieved to have your clothes back on. Home and bed—that sounds nice. Of course, Michael might be there. You're not sure if that would be good or bad. Peter would be safer than Michael—at least Peter's single. And presumably straight. You stop at the café on the way home, but there's no sign of him. Neither Michael nor Jamie is home when you get in, so you end up curled in bed, reading a novel, until you fall asleep.

• PLEASE TURN TO PAGE 142.

It's tempting to just dive in—when you slide a hand up under your loose skirt, you find your panties are already damp, and you pull them off. You could climb up onto him, stroke that cock until it's nice and hard, maybe lick it a little, and then ride him until you both come. But really, talking first seems like a better plan.

→

Y ou climb onto the bed, undo the gag, bend down, and drop
a kiss on Peter's lips. "Hey there. How you doing?"

"Good." He says it softly, uncertainly. He doesn't sound
entirely convinced.

He's sweating a little in the warm room, and you gently brush
your hand across his damp forehead. "So," you say quietly, "I want
you to tell me exactly why you're all tied up here like this. It's a
lovely present, but what's the occasion?"

"Well, you said that you wanted to do this . . ." He sounds
almost defensive, like he wants you to think this is all your idea.
You're not about to let him get away with that!

"Hey—*I* was thinking maybe more of the tying-up stuff, or you
might bend me over your knee and spank me a couple times. Some
of the stuff you've laid out here is intense. Is this what you want?" You
try to keep your voice calm, nonjudgmental. If he does want to be
whipped, then as a good girlfriend, you should probably try to oblige,
right? The idea is a little intriguing—you might even enjoy it.

He's quiet, not saying anything. Sometimes he gets quiet like
this, too embarrassed to tell you what he wants. Usually you coax
it out of him, which can take a while, but maybe you have a short-
cut available tonight.

"Peter, I'm *ordering* you to tell me what you want. Right now!"
You make your voice snap, and even with the blindfold on, you can
tell that he's startled. He opens his mouth, and the words start
spilling out.

"I—I want you to fuck me. In the ass." He's blushing again, a
reddish hue spreading under his dark skin. It's sexy, with the blindfold and all. He looks very vulnerable, very *fuckable,* somehow.

You sit back on your heels for a minute, considering. You decide to leave the blindfold on—it makes him look so helpless. The wrist restraints, too. But the gag should definitely stay off. If you're going to do this, you want to be sure you can hear his responses, know if you're going too slow or too fast.

Most of this junk you don't need, and you sweep it off the bed, letting it clatter onto the wooden floor. Just the dildo and the lube and the harness. The harness looks kind of tricky.

You're definitely overdressed for this venture; you could take off your skirt, but you're probably going to be working pretty hard, getting sweaty. You quickly strip off everything so that you're as naked as Peter is. Then you fumble with the harness and the dildo until you figure out exactly how it works—a hole for the dildo, straps around your hips and thighs that you can adjust to fit you exactly. In a surprisingly short time, you're sporting an attractive leather harness and a jutting cock.

"Roll over." You're pleased with how firm that sounded, like a command. He must want at least a little of the domination stuff or he wouldn't have done this, right? And he certainly rolls over quickly, if awkwardly, with both his wrists still fastened up above his head. Now his ass, tight and firm, is completely available to you.

You pour some lube onto your right hand, really soak a couple of fingers. You drizzle lube onto his asshole, too; it's cold enough to make him jerk, but then he settles down again. He's breathing heavy enough that you can hear him, either tense or turned on. Or both. You start with one finger, pressing it up against his asshole, gently. You slide it back and forth a bit, and even that's enough to get a reaction out of him; he moves his butt up, just enough to make it clear he likes it, that he wants more. You push your finger in, and it goes in easily up to the first knuckle. Peter makes a low sound, almost a groan. You pull the finger out, then push it in again, back and forth, pushing a little farther each time while he makes tiny, involuntary motions under your hand. It's sexy, watching him move, listening to the small sounds he can't help making. You're getting turned on, too, and you reach down for your clit, only to find that you can't reach it. It's buried under the dildo's base. So you slide a few fingers into your wet pussy instead, pumping them in and out, slowly, in time with the motions of your right hand.

Before long, he's opened up enough to easily take your entire forefinger, so you add another finger, dripping some more lube on. You push two fingers in, and this time it goes slower, with more resistance. You just keep adding more lube and pushing, firmly but slowly. You don't want to rush this—if you do, you'll hurt him and he'll tighten up and you'll hurt him even more. You remember that much from the stories you've read. Though all of those had been about a man fucking a woman. It's fun turning it around like this; there's a strange thrill to having him under your hand, having the power to hurt him but not using it. Normally, there's no way you could hurt him during sex—he's strong enough that you can flail around as much as you want and he can pin you down and wait for you to calm. You've been enjoying that, the uncontrolled passion of it, but there's a different pleasure here, in taking infinite care, making sure that everything you do feels very, very good. It must be something like the way a man feels when he has sex with a woman who's a virgin. You feel strong, concerned, protective. It's a powerful feeling. And it's totally turning you on. Your cunt is dripping wet.

You're pumping two fingers in and out of him now, steadily. Peter's arching his ass to meet you, and tiny whimpers escape him when your fingers fill him fully. He's loosened up; he's as ready as you're going to make him. Now it's time to pull out the big guns. You pull your fingers completely out with a small pop, and straddle his thighs, your dildo poised and ready just above his ass.

The dildo is a smooth shaft; you lube it up really well and drip more lube onto his asshole, pushing some in with a finger. Then you place the head of the dildo against his asshole and push with your hips. The tip slides in easily, but then you hit resistance—firm resistance. The dildo isn't huge, but it's definitely thicker than two fingers. You pull out and push forward again, tentatively, and again you hit a wall, not even an inch in. It's frustrating—you want to be deep inside him, fucking him. You try pushing, leaning forward so your weight is helping to push it into his ass. Peter makes a muffled sound, a yelp, and you freeze.

"Peter?" Did you hurt him?

"I'm OK. Just—take it slow. Please?"

"Definitely slow. *Infinitely* slow. Just stay with me, baby." You pull out smoothly, then very slowly push in again. A bit farther this time, and Peter makes another sound but doesn't say stop—in fact, after a minute, he raises his ass an inch or so, inviting more. You rock in and out, working your way in as slowly as you can. You're both sweaty and dripping now, but that can only help, and you go deeper and deeper until finally, *finally,* it's all the way in, it's buried completely in his ass, and your breasts are soft against his back, your hips are pressed up against his ass-cheeks, and you suddenly realize that this is a very strange place to be.

Strange, but good. It's good to wrap your arms around Peter now, to hold him tight. You rest against his long, lean, strong body for a moment. You kiss the skin of his back, a few small, fluttery kisses. Then you take a deep breath and start to move again.

Slowly at first, in and out. The first time you go back in, there's some resistance, but as you keep moving, it gets smoother, easier. And from the small sounds he's making, the grunts of satisfaction getting deeper and louder, he's not going to last much longer. You're not going to come from this, but the pounding of his ass against your hips, the dildo pressing back against your clit, does feel good. Very good. Not good enough to make you come, but good enough to keep you nicely excited and motivated to keep up the motion, pumping in and out of your boyfriend's ass. You like the way that sounds in your head—*your boyfriend's ass.* It's sort of dirty, and definitely sexy. Your hands braced on his back, his breath coming heavy and hard as you pound into him, as your hips slam against his ass, your cock drives deep inside him, and he's close now, you can hear it, the low growls getting louder and louder, so you speed it up, you dig your nails into his back and really give it to him, pounding as hard as you can, over and over and over until finally he comes, spurting wildly onto the sheets.

Maybe being the top means that you can make him sleep in the wet spot. . . .

• PLEASE TURN TO PAGE 196.

You make your excuses to the hosts and ask them to tell Rose you're leaving. You'd tell her yourself, but she looks busy, in the midst of a threesome with a man and a woman. The woman has her mouth on Rose's breast; the man is sliding a condom over his erect cock. It looks like he'll be sliding into Rose next, and you don't want to interrupt.

When you get home, it takes a while before you get up the nerve to call Peter. Rose has a list of names and numbers on the fridge, and Peter's is at the top of the list. It's past midnight when you finally dial his number; you know you should wait until morning, but you just can't. You need to know if you have a shot with him.

"Hey, Peter. It's Kathryn."

"Kathryn?" He sounds bewildered. Also a little fuzzy.

"I'm sorry, did I wake you?" Of course you did. Idiot. Why didn't you wait until morning?

"No, no. I was just in the middle of working on a problem. It's fine. I usually don't go to bed until much later."

"Oh." That's good then. God, just listening to his voice, low and sweet, makes your pussy cream. That guy at the party left you high and dry; you're aching for it now. Can Peter hear it in your voice? "Well, I was wondering—is there any chance you'd like to get together with me sometime?" Boldness, that's the key. Just dive right in. Worst he can do is say no.

"Really? But—but I didn't think you were interested."

"I've reconsidered. I'm definitely interested." You are so very interested. Your nipples are sore and you can't help sliding a hand down inside your panties, rub a finger across your wet clit. How bold can you be? You drop your voice, make it low, soft, and sexy.

"In fact, if you'd be interested in coming by tonight, that'd be OK with me."

"Um, I'm not sure that would be a good idea." Shit, you pushed too hard! Is he going to pull away entirely? That would be so damn frustrating. "But sure, I'd like to see you again. I'll call you tomorrow?"

"Tomorrow would be great." Tomorrow will be fine.

"Great. Good night, Kathryn."

"Good night, Peter." Sleep tight. You hang up the phone.

→

Y ou go to bed more than a little frustrated, but pleased, too. It's kind of nice that he's not rushing things—it's romantic. You touch yourself slowly, giving yourself small orgasms until you fall asleep, thinking about Peter. Sort of geeky, surprisingly intense, intriguing. And still really hot.

He calls the next morning, right before noon, and asks whether you might be free during the day today or tomorrow. He wants to take you to Fisherman's Wharf, maybe out to see Alcatraz. Your girlfriends back home would have told you to make him wait a bit, but you don't really want to. You want to see him as soon as possible. So you tell him you're free today, and that you can be ready in half an hour. He warns you to wear a heavy sweater, since it'll be chilly on the wharf and out at the prison. It's sweet, the way he thinks about your comfort. You like that.

The wharf is a lot of fun—eating clam chowder out of bread bowls, strolling along hand in hand, listening to the street musicians, laughing at the tourists with their massive cameras. You're not a tourist anymore, you're a local. This is your city.

The mood shifts when you get out to Alcatraz; the cells with their recorded voices of long-gone prisoners are almost unbearably sad. One of them talks about how, on warm summer nights, the water would carry across to them the sounds from the wharf—cheerful music, girls' voices. It almost makes you want to cry, and Peter puts an arm around you as you walk through the tour. It helps.

On the way back, you're standing alone at the rail with him, the wind ruffling in your hair. His right arm is around you still, and you lean up against his long body—partly for warmth, partly because you want to. He's talking about swimming—he's part of some crazy group that swims in the Bay in the middle of winter. Nutty. But he's all excited about it, and he's waving his left arm around enthusiastically. You turn slightly in his arms to watch his animated face, and he looks down at you, grinning. It would be a perfect moment for a kiss, and you lean toward him. But nothing. He just keeps talking, all the way back to the wharf. What's wrong with this boy? He seems to like spending time with you—why doesn't he kiss you?

You have a yummy dinner at a Jamaican place, and you're even brave enough to try the curried goat, which is surprisingly tasty and only a little too spicy for you. Sally would be proud. Again Peter walks you home, but this time he doesn't even walk you upstairs, almost as if he doesn't trust himself to kiss you at the apartment door. A quick kiss downstairs, and then he's gone, leaving you to climb the five flights alone. This is getting annoying.

• PLEASE TURN TO PAGE 188.

You rest one more moment in John's arms, then, a little regretfully, step out of them. Maybe John's changed, but that doesn't mean you want to go with him. That part of your life is over.

"I'm sorry, Johnny. I think it's great that you're changing, that you're willing to try new things. I hope it goes well for you. But I'm happy here. This is my home now."

"But what about us? Katie . . ."

"There is no *us,* Johnny." How can you make this clear to him? You don't want him hanging around like a puppy dog. "I'm seeing someone else now, and he's a stripper. He's incredible in bed. He does things for me that you never could."

John looks stunned, shell-shocked. The buzzer sounds. You say, "I'm sorry—I have to go. That's him." You hesitate. He looks so sad, so pathetic. "If you want to spend the night on the couch, you can." Michael's at the door, buzzing your date in through the downstairs gate.

"We really don't have a shot, do we?" John's voice is plaintive but already hopeless. He knows this isn't going to work.

"No, Johnny." You say it as firmly as you can.

"Then I'd best get back home again." He turns away and walks down the hall. You follow, walking slowly. By the time you get to the end of the hall, the door's already open and Stripper-guy's waiting there. John reaches out and takes his hand, shakes it solemnly. "You take good care of our Katie." Your date looks bewildered, but before he says anything, John lets go, walks down the stairs, disappearing into the night.

You smile up at the stripper—Alex, that was his name. You remember it now. "Don't worry about it. A ghost from my past."

"You OK?" Alex looks worried, frown lines marring his beautiful face. You stretch up on tiptoes and kiss him lightly, until the lines disappear.

"I'm great—ready and raring to go."

And you are. You're sorry for John, sorry he came all this way for no reward. But you're happy for yourself; this is where you want to be, and you're doing what you want to be doing. A great city, a great job, great roommates—and as many dates as you care to go on. Maybe tonight you'll take Alex to bed. Maybe this will turn out to be true love—or just excellent sex. You take his hand in yours and lead him firmly out the door, into the expectant city.

THE END

Y ou smile at Rose. "Thanks, that was fun."

"For me, too, chica."

"So, what happens next?"

"Well, usually you just wander around. Talk to people. If you see someone you like, you can invite them to do something. If someone invites you to do something, you can say yes or no. It's all very casual, friendly. You'll be fine." Rose is already standing up, her eyes across the room, fixed on a pretty redheaded girl standing alone in the corner, looking back at Rose. "Come and get me if you need anything—or you can always ask Carol." And she walks away, toward the redhead, leaving you alone.

You're not quite sure what to do, so you remain cross-legged a minute, just sitting on the floor and watching. This is all so strange. Most people are paired up right now, but there are some single people wandering around, and off in a corner is a growing pile, three or four people all tangled up together. What would it be like to have so many hands on you? Would it be exciting or just creepy?

A hand touches your shoulder, startling you. You twist around to see a rather good-looking man behind you. Dark brown hair, skin so pale it almost glows in this dim light. Powerfully built, broad shoulders tapering to a narrow waist. And he's naked, with the thickest, longest cock you've ever seen. Honestly, you'd sort of thought that mostly unattractive people went to sex parties, people who didn't get much sex otherwise; this guy could go to any bar and have his pick of women. What brought him here?

He bends down and whispers in your ear. "You're very beautiful. I'd like to tie you up with silk scarves. I'd like to lick you until you come. I'd like to bend you over my knee and spank you until your ass turns nice and red. I want your soft, wet mouth on my cock. I want to fuck you hard, pretty lady. I want to fuck you all night long."

Oof. This guy doesn't play around. It's definitely sexy to have someone talking so directly about sex, about what he wants to do with your body. But it's shocking, too—this guy doesn't know you at all! You don't know him! For a moment, you feel confused; you can't tell if you're turned on or repulsed. What are you going to do?

- *If you keep talking to him,* PLEASE TURN TO PAGE 207.

- *If you turn him down,* PLEASE TURN TO PAGE 213.

Y ou pick up a cup of hot chocolate and close your hands around it, grateful for the warmth. You start to sit down, but before you can, Michael intervenes.

"Honey, you're shivering. Why, that little sweater is drenched. You really have to get that off—you could catch your death! Didn't anyone tell you how to dress in San Francisco? It's all about layers! Rosie, grab her a towel, sweetie?"

He takes the cup out of your hands, and his hands are on your sweater, pulling it up and off your head before you can protest. It's not a big deal, though—you're wearing a tank top underneath, so you're still decent, and besides, he's gay. He's gay! So it's like he's not really a guy, right? He couldn't care less that your heart's beating faster at the accidental brush of his knuckles against your waist, your shoulders. There's not a single hair on his upper body, as far as you can see. Maybe he shaves it all off?

In the midst of this, Rose must have gotten a towel, because now there's one wrapped around you, and Michael is vigorously rubbing it over your arms, your back, toweling off your blond hair. You'd cut it just before coming out here; it used to hang to your waist, but now it swings just to shoulder length. He doesn't linger where you'd like him to—on your sensitive neck, your spine—and he makes only the briefest brush of the towel across your breasts. Just enough for your nipples to get hard, though he certainly wouldn't have noticed. You *hope* he didn't notice. When he finishes drying you off, he pushes down on your shoulders, gently but firmly, and your legs fold, landing you on the futon couch. He puts the cup back in your hands—"Now, drink it all." And you do, trying to remember to breathe.

Rose perches on the scarred wooden coffee table, a little too close. She's still not wearing much of anything, though she's picked up a red sweater and is holding it cradled in her hands. "So, Kathryn, Sally told me that you had the money for the first two months' rent saved up, but that you'd need to get a job here? Are you looking for anything in particular? Have any skills?"

"Oh, here's a check." You fumble in your wet jeans, finally pulling out your wallet and getting out a slightly damp check. A thousand dollars—you'd never written a check that large before. The place you shared in college cost you only $220 a month. You've never actually earned enough to afford the rents here, but Sally did say that pay was higher out here, too. "Well, I can type, and I've always liked computers. I can hand-code HTML. I don't know how to really program, though; I was an English major."

Michael curls onto the futon next to you, his bare knees brushing your jeans-covered thighs. He looks worried. "It's not a great time to try to break into computers here—the job market's really tight since the dot-com crash. A few years ago, you could've easily gotten a Web design gig, but these days, everyone's a designer and no one wants to hire unless you have some advanced skills and solid work experience. You could probably get something in tech writing. Kind of the bottom of the barrel, but not a bad place to start, and it doesn't require much in the way of computer skills. I think I know a contracting group that's actually looking for help on a rush gig they picked up— I could try to get you an interview, if you want. . . ."

→

"Sure, if you can make a call, that would be great." It's awfully nice of him, and it makes you feel a little better about the whole job thing. You hadn't really been sure where to start looking.

"Mike's a tech writer," Rose says. "He knows all about that stuff. Bores me to tears, I have to say—I tried it for a while, but the money's a lot better in stripping, and it's easier to fit around my schedule. Hey, you're not interested in trying that, are you? The Lusty Lady is pretty decent—we're woman-owned, unionized and everything. They're having amateur night tomorrow, basically an open audition. From what I can see, you've got a great body!"

Gorgeous *Rose* thinks you have a great body? You're blushing as her eyes sweep up and down, pausing to consider your rather large breasts. The damp tank top doesn't hide much. You'd always found your breasts sort of a nuisance, but maybe for a stripper they'd be an asset. Rose can't really see much in the way of details, but you do work out; you're pretty trim. But don't men want someone sexier as a stripper? Would they think *you* were sexy? My God, are you actually thinking seriously about this? You did take a lot of dance classes in college, so that part shouldn't be too hard. But taking off your clothes? For money?

"Um, I'll think about it, OK?" Thinking doesn't commit you to anything.

"Sure thing—but be done thinking by tomorrow night at eight. That's when we'd need to be there. Do you have anything sexy to wear? Black lace panties, cowboy boots, latex bra, feather boa, Catholic-schoolgirl outfit?" She's pulling on her clothes while she talks—the red sweater goes over a perfectly normal short black skirt—she must keep her costumes at the club. Black knee-high socks, tall black boots. You want boots like that.

"Not really." You have a couple pairs of jeans and some shirts and sweaters. Sneakers. All your underwear is plain black cotton—comfortable, practical, but clearly inadequate.

"We can go shopping tomorrow, if you want. OK, must dash, my sweets." She blows you a kiss and is gone, the door swinging closed behind her, leaving you alone with gorgeous, untouchable Michael.

Michael smiles at you. It's the kind of smile that could make a girl melt. He has very white teeth, perfectly even. Lots of dental work, maybe. It looks good. "I think you're gonna fit right in here, Kathryn. Is it always Kathryn? Not Kate, or Katie?"

"Usually Kathryn, but I'm flexible."

He grins. "Flexible is good." He makes it sound like much more than you'd meant it to be. He's gay. Must remember that he's gay. And he has a serious boyfriend. They're probably practically married. Maybe they are married. Can gays get married? He's still sitting awfully close to you, still wearing only bike shorts. Still smiling, almost gazing into your eyes. You could happily gaze right back into his, but instead, you break eye contact and look away.

It's the first chance you've had to really look around the place. Rose is a little whirlwind—when she's around, rushing here and there, it's difficult to focus on anything else. Nice high ceilings, with arched moldings. Clean white walls. The futon you're sitting on is dark blue and battered but comfortable, under two long windows that look out onto the street. Along another wall is a wide wooden bench—no, not just a bench, it's a church pew. What's a church pew doing in an apartment?

"You like it?" Michael says, following your glance. "Jamie found it; he's fabulous with rummage sales. Drives all over the place on the weekends; he calls it hunting for treasure. I never got into it myself, but sometimes I go with him. The things we do for love . . ."

"It's gorgeous." And it is, you have to admit, though as a good Episcopalian girl who went to church every single Sunday back home, you're a little shocked. Still, you can imagine how much fun it would be, driving from sale to sale, finding this gem. You wonder if Jamie would mind if you tagged along sometime. Lush crimson pillows are scattered across it; much more comfortable-looking than the polished bare wood. There's not a lot of other furniture in the room: wooden coffee table, worn enough that you feel comfortable pushing off your wet sneakers and resting your damp sock-clad feet on it. Tall bookshelves cover the other two walls, crammed full with a jumble of books. No single chairs, just two battered love seats across from the pew; it would be difficult to keep someone from sitting next to you, if he wanted to. His thigh against yours. Michael's thighs are nice and firm. If he were sitting there, next to you on the pew, his skin would be warm, and his breath would be almost close enough to feel.

You stand up abruptly. "Could I get a tour?" You do *not* need to get a crush on your gay roommate.

"Sure thing—and then we can start dinner." Michael unfolds himself from the futon. He's quite tall, maybe six inches taller than you, and you're not short. "Jamie should be home any minute—

he's the real cook in the house. I usually prep things for him, though. How are you at chopping onions?"

"I can do onions." You're oddly relieved at the thought of chopping onions. It's perfectly domestic, the kind of thing that you used to do back home, in your mother's kitchen. That's a nice safe thing to do, maybe sautéing them and adding chopped garlic, tomatoes, a few bell peppers . . .

"Great! He e-mailed and said he was planning on Vietnamese tonight. You like Vietnamese?"

"Sure. Sure, Vietnamese sounds great." And just like that, your stomach turns queasy. You've never had Vietnamese in your life. You've had Chinese, Italian, a little Mexican, and plain old boring American. What the hell is in Vietnamese food? Snails? Jellyfish? You know it's childish, but somehow the thought of it makes you want to curl up in a dark corner and cry.

• PLEASE TURN TO PAGE 47.

You're back on the bus again, riding home to Greendale. The rain is disappearing, and a bright sun is taking over the sky. At every stop, more brown and black people get off; more white people get on. You feel safer. Your folks will be glad to see you; maybe John will take you back. If you're very sweet to him, maybe he'll understand that you never meant to hurt him. Maybe you'll get your blue house with the white picket fence, your two children, your big Saint Bernard. Indiana's a good place to raise kids; it's clean and safe.

A ghost of hot chocolate lingers on your tongue, dark and sweet as sin. Soon it'll be gone, though, just a brief taste of a place full of crazy people, a place where you never really belonged.

It'll be good to be home again.

THE END

Monday you work an extra-long day so you can feel justified in taking Tuesday off. You like setting your own schedule like this—hooray for tech writing! Peter teaches Tuesday mornings, so he has to work Monday, grading exams. But you talk on the phone Monday night for a couple of hours. You even tell him about John. You enjoy the conversation—he's a good listener, and you get the feeling that you could tell him anything.

On Tuesday, he arrives around noon, and you walk to Golden Gate Park. It's a beautifully sunny day, unseasonably warm. You're in a clingy white T-shirt and jeans, and he's wearing only a thin white button-down shirt and khakis. As you walk, you can almost see his muscles moving under his clothes. Yummy. You stop at the edge of the park for Ben & Jerry's and argue mildly about the relative merits of Cherry Garcia and Chunky Monkey. Even though Peter doesn't appreciate the wonder that is Cherry Garcia, you're still having a great time with him. He gives you a bite of his cone, which is dripping down onto his hand—you fight the temptation to start licking him clean. There are people all around you, and it probably wouldn't be appropriate. You're not sure you care, though.

You spend an hour in the Asian art museum, which is impressive, but you can't stay inside on a beautiful day like today. You enter the tea garden and wander around its winding paths. There's a bridge that's strangely high, almost vertical, and it takes Peter some effort to convince you to try crossing it. But once you start, it's easy. You pause to admire the great golden-orange koi swimming serenely just under the surface of the water. Peter says that they're considered wise, and you can see that. They're so peaceful. But you're not feeling peaceful, or wise. Peter's hand is holding yours, his head is bent next to yours—no one else is around, and it's a perfect time for a kiss. You want a kiss, damn it—one of his amazing kisses. But he hasn't kissed you yet today, and it's becoming clear that he's not going to kiss you anytime soon. If you want a kiss, you're going to have to start one yourself.

You turn your head, tilt it up a little, and kiss him.

He almost pulls away, but then he leans into it; he brings up one hand to entangle your hair, holding you there gently. Peter's lips move lightly on yours—you're almost breathing in sync, and it's a good thing his hand is holding you there, because you're getting dizzy. There's something amazing about Peter's kisses. He's as intense about kissing as he was at dinner the other night, when he was talking about math. When he's kissing you, it's like there's nothing else in the world but you, and he's going to focus every bit of attention he has on you. It's intoxicating. One of his hands slides down your body to the small of your back, pulling you closer until you're pressed against him. You can feel him, hard against your hip. If just kissing does that to him, then what'll happen if you do more?

When you finally break, he looks startled, his eyes wide. Should you apologize? He sure seemed like he enjoyed the kiss. You start to apologize: "I'm sorry—didn't you want to?"

"No, no. I did want to. Very much. Um, do you mind if we find someplace more private?"

You don't mind that at all. Maybe you'll get to realize that fantasy you had when he was walking you home from the coffee shop—sex with Peter in the park, in the sunlight. You take his hand, and he leads you out of the Japanese garden into the larger park.

The park's huge, and it doesn't take long before you're in a small wooded dell, well screened from casual passersby. Anyone who made his way in here would almost have to be looking for the same thing you are, so hopefully he'll turn right around and leave you alone if he does. It makes you nervous, making out in public. But it's exciting, too—what if someone did catch you? What if he stayed there and watched? Just the thought makes you even wetter than you already were.

You're kissing Peter again, pulling him down to lie on the grass with you. The sun's shafting down through the trees, and it's warm here—almost too warm. Warm enough that when his hands wander down to your breasts and start, tentatively, to caress them, you reach down and pull your T-shirt up, over your head, leaving you in just a lacy pale blue bra. With a front clasp. Peter looks startled again—maybe you're going too fast for him. But he doesn't turn down the invitation; his hands curve around your breasts; his fingers rub your nipples through the lace, then he unclasps the bra, looking at your face to be sure this is what you want. You do. He peels the bra back, freeing your breasts. He touches them gently, his fingers moving so lightly over the skin that it makes you shiver, makes you want to scream. But you need to be quiet here, very, very quiet. You don't want to actually lure people in here.

You close your eyes and arch under the touch of his hands; his fingers feel so good. They wander up and down your torso, coming back to your breasts, then wander away again. He bends down and starts kissing you again, not intense kisses like last time, but butterfly kisses that start at your mouth, then travel to your ear, your neck, your shoulder. They almost tickle, but not quite. They're something between a kiss and a lick, barely wet. And then he's kissing the upper curve of your breast, circling down and around the nipple, and now you really are arching, your hands in his hair holding him down, mutely begging him to please, please put his mouth on your nipple, and when he finally does, it's an explosion, it's like a mouthful of ice cream on a painfully hot day. You're biting your lip to keep quiet, but when Peter starts sucking, still so gently, on your nipple, small sounds rise out of you, rising in your throat and being swallowed again. He can hear you, and when you open your eyes for a second, he looks up and smiles.

He goes back to sucking on your nipples—first one, then the other. Your hands pull out his shirt and manage to unbutton it enough that you can feel some of his bare skin against yours. Your hands roam restlessly across what you can reach of his body. It's frustrating, how little you can reach, but you don't want him to stop what he's doing. One of his legs is between yours now, and you wrap your legs around it and start to move, up and down, humping his leg like a dog in heat, but you can't help it. You want more. And you're going to have to move to get it, since it looks like Peter will cheerfully suck your nipples all afternoon.

You put your hands on his chest, and he stops what he's doing, raises his head inquisitively. You push, just a little, and he rolls back; you roll with him, so that you end up on top. Your breasts are hanging over his face, and you're on your knees above him, your pussy up around his stomach. That's not so helpful. You slide down, just enough that your jeans-covered crotch is resting on his hard cock. That feels better. That feels really good. He's lying back, letting you direct the show. You take his hands in yours, bring them back to your breasts. You're sitting upright now, rocking slowly back and forth in the sunshine, while he kneads your breasts, squeezing the nipples. You feel shameless—and his cock feels so good, even through layers of fabric. Rubbing against your clit, over and over, while sparks shoot down from your nipples to your pussy. You don't know if he's enjoying this, but at this point you don't much care, as long as he keeps going, keeps letting you ride him, as you get closer and closer . . .

And then you hear voices. Loud voices.

You're tempted to just keep going, but Peter rolls you over quickly so his body is shielding your naked breasts. You can't see anyone, but you hear the voices abruptly stopping, a girl's giggle, a rustle in the grass as they turn and walk away. You're tempted to giggle, too, until you see Peter's face, which has gone almost ashen. He looks incredibly embarrassed.

"I'm so sorry, Kathryn. I didn't think anyone would come in here." He's handing you your bra, your T-shirt.

"It's no big deal. I don't really care if some strangers see my breasts. Besides, wasn't it exciting?" You're still excited, very excited. You want to take this further now, unbutton his pants maybe, pull out his cock. If only you'd worn a skirt instead of jeans. You have to learn to plan better for these park trips.

"Too exciting for me, I'm afraid." He tries to grin, but it's entirely unconvincing. His color is returning to normal, but he still looks anything but turned on. He's buttoning up his shirt, tucking it in. And there's no bulge in his pants now—he's clearly going to need some more recovery time. You sigh under your breath and pull your bra back on. His eyes watch your breasts as you cover them, so it's not entirely hopeless.

"Maybe we should go someplace more private than this?" If you can get him back to his place, the train ride should give him plenty of time to recover.

"Sounds good." He leans over and drops a light kiss on your lips. Peter seems relieved that you don't want to push it, but you don't know him that well yet—maybe he's not relieved. Maybe he's disappointed. It's strange, being the sexually aggressive one. You're not quite sure how far to push anything. But God, surviving an hour on public transit when you're *this* horny is not going to be easy.

You're good on the bus, but when you get on the train across the Bay, you start getting restless. You're sitting in a rear seat, up against a window. No one's standing in the car—no one's sitting closer than three seats away. Perfect for some preliminary fooling around. You could reach out and start rubbing his cock through his pants. That might be too much. But surely he won't object to anything you do to yourself? It's tempting. . . .

Peter's quiet for once, watching the tunnel flicker past outside the window. You lean up against him and slowly start caressing one of your own breasts through your shirt. You're just small enough that the seat blocks the view of anyone else in the car—as long as they don't stand up. You can't quite believe you're doing this, but it's awfully exciting. You're still wound up from the park, and the movement of the train, with its steady rumbling, adds to your excitement. And to be honest, the thought that someone might see you doesn't hurt. You rub a nipple until it gets erect, then squeeze it, gently at first, then harder. Sometimes you like to squeeze them really hard. You pinch your nipple hard, and a quick breath comes out of you. That's when Peter notices what you're doing.

"Kathryn!" He keeps his voice very soft, but he's clearly not happy with you. "Please stop that." His hand on your shoulder squeezes once, almost hard enough to hurt.

"Are you sure?" You look up at him, licking your lips, and let your other hand drift over to his leg, coming to rest on his thigh.

"I'm sure. I would love you to do that, but not now, not here. There are all kinds of things I'd love to do with you, but please, can't we wait until we have some privacy?" His hand is hovering over yours, as if he wants to remove it from his thigh but isn't quite sure how you'd react.

"What if I don't want to stop?" You tilt your head up and whisper the next words into his ear. "What if I want to keep going until I come? You left me hanging, after all; maybe you owe me." That's not fair, but sex isn't about being fair, is it? And you are *so* damn horny.

"It's up to you, but I really wish you wouldn't do this." Peter's forehead is all scrunched up; he looks pretty unhappy. But maybe that's nervousness—he was too nervous to kiss you in the park, after all. And once you kissed him, that turned out great. If you keep pushing, maybe he'll enjoy it. Does he secretly want you to push him? It can be scary, doing new things. Maybe he's a guy who wants a woman to tell him what to do. And you're so horny! It's tempting—you could zip open your jeans, slip them down enough to slide a finger onto your clit. That's all you'd need to come right now. He wouldn't stop you, and if you did put your hand on his cock, start rubbing, surely he'd go along with it. Don't guys always want sex? That's what everyone says. . . .

- *If you go for it and put your hand on his cock,* PLEASE TURN TO PAGE 136.

- *If you give in to Peter's request and take your hand off your nipple,* PLEASE TURN TO PAGE 150.

You fall asleep eventually, before waking up to do it all over again. Only this time, you're the one tied up. By the time you've finished, you're both shaking; there's something tremendously intimate about what you've done. If you can trust Peter with this, maybe you can trust him with a whole lot more.

In the next few days and weeks, the sex feels different. More emotional, more intense. You've pushed through to a different level, and it feels amazing.

Is it true love? Hard to say—it's been only a few weeks. But recently, every once in a while, you've felt the urge to tell Peter you love him. Maybe he'll beat you to it, sometime soon. Right now you feel pretty blissful. Being with Peter makes you happy. Having a great job makes you happy. Living in one of the world's coolest cities, with cool roommates—that makes you happy, too. There are a gazillion restaurants you haven't tried yet, there's always a good movie playing somewhere, and the sex-toy shops here are both friendly and well lighted. Those have to be the signs of a healthy, happy city.

You've come a long way from Indiana in just a little while. It wasn't so long ago that you walked away from a extended engagement to your high school sweetheart, the classic happy ending that all the girls dreamed of. But it wasn't the right happy ending for you, and you have no desire to move back to Indiana. Maybe one of these days you'll go home for a visit—maybe, if Peter's still around at Christmas, you might even bring him home with you. You should probably tell your mother about him first, so she doesn't have a heart attack when she sees him. Sally's sure to like him, and you're going to like introducing him to John. . . .

Peter's dozing now, curled up behind you, breathing softly on your neck. You shift a little, and he wakes up, tightening his arms around you, pressing his hips and hardening cock up against your ass. He drops a soft kiss on your neck, and you shiver. You're not sure what the future will bring, but it's looking nice and bright right now. And when he whispers, very quietly, "I love you," into your tangled hair, you think that, just maybe, you might have found a happy ending after all.

THE END

Rose makes a little sound in her throat and then leans forward again. You kiss her as well as you know how. Not too dry, not too slobbery. Just soft and intense, your mouth slightly open. Her tongue brushes against your lips. Your tongue lingers on hers, explores her lips, her tongue, her teeth. Sitting like this is awkward, and you rise up, pulling her with you until you're both on your knees, and now you can easily undo her tie. It's a good thing you've had practice with a man. You slip off the tie and start unbuttoning her shirt. Only a few buttons and her breasts are exposed, small and perfect. You hesitate then, not sure what to do with your hands. You're still kissing, and she's unbuttoning the last two buttons on your shirt, pushing it off your shoulders to fall on the floor, leaving you in just bra and panties. You have a moment of nervousness—there are so many people in the room, are they looking at you? What do they think of your body? But then Rose kisses you harder, her hands gently roaming up and down the skin of your back, tracing a line along your spine, and you shiver and stop thinking about anybody but her. You touch a hand to her breast—you're touching a woman's breast! Not your own! It's incredibly soft, softer than any man's chest. And when you tentatively slide your fingers up and caress a nipple, it turns hard under your fingers, and Rose makes another lost sound, helplessly.

She's incredibly responsive: when your mouth moves away from hers, down to kiss her neck, her whole body shivers and leans into your kiss. You want to kiss every inch of her, to explore her properly. You try to undo the belt that holds up her schoolgirl skirt, tugging impatiently at it when it resists you, and she giggles as she reaches to do it for you. It's that giggle that gets you—it's endearing. Ever since you met Rose, you've been amazed at how cheerful she is, how energetic and bubbly. You can be a bit moody yourself; you spent most of the month before you left Indiana in a miserable funk, staring out your bedroom window and wishing things were different. You can't imagine staying mopey with Rose around—her enthusiasm is infectious and irresistible. Look at where you are now: nearly naked at a sex party, fooling around with a nearly naked woman. Rose has pushed off her shoes, and now she's just wearing the knee-high socks and the gold cross. Your knees are getting sore, so you tug at her, just enough that you both tumble down to the cushioned floor. You land on your sides, facing each other. Her eyes are tawny brown, streaked with gold. You hadn't looked at her eyes properly before. They're entrancing.

You don't want to give Rose time to reconsider this, or to think about her nutty anti-roommate policy. So you quickly go back to kissing her. When in doubt, kissing always seems like a good bet. You tug the bands off her braids—they're cute braids, but you want to run your fingers through her hair. She helps you unbraid them, and soon her hair is curling loose and luscious around her shoulders, her breasts, your breasts, which are half an inch away from hers. The hair tickles, but it feels good, too. She reaches behind you and pulls you close so she can unhook your bra. She does it so smoothly—men always fumble it. Before you can blink, it's off, and she's cradling your breasts in her small hands. You never thought of them as all that large, but they look huge in her hands. She slides down just enough to take a nipple in her mouth. God. Her eager wet mouth moves hungrily against your skin, licking, then sucking, then playfully biting at the nipple, making you squirm among the cushions. You want to return the favor, but you can't reach her tits with your mouth. Instead, you reach down with both hands, caress the skin of her breasts, trace the valley between them, mark spirals around them until you reach her nipples, dark and erect, nipples much thicker than yours, and very sensitive. When you finally reach them and squeeze gently, Rose moans into your flesh, and the sound pulses through you, running right from your breast down to your pussy.

You want to touch her, to taste her. You slide down, reach for her naked pussy. She stops you with a quick hand on your arm: "Gloves, remember." Right. Safe sex only, or you get thrown out. And you really don't want to stop things right now! Everything you need is in easy reach, and you quickly slide gloves on. What you really want is to taste her, but this will have to do for now. You put a hand on her thigh and she opens up for you, lying back in the cushions, eyes wide. You slide a finger into her, and she whimpers, arching. Back and forth—she's so wet, she takes two fingers, three. Easily. You wonder if she could take more—four fingers, your whole fist. You've heard of fisting but never thought of letting someone do it to you. You were sure it would hurt. Now you're not so sure, but you're also not confident enough to go there now. This is enough, this is plenty. Your fingers pumping in and out of Rose, your other hand busy on her clit, touching her just the way you like to be touched, and she is whimpering and shaking under you, her slim body is arching up so beautifully, and you can't help bending over to take a thick brown nipple in your mouth, you can't help biting down, just the right amount, and that's when she comes, comes hard, comes around your fingers so hard that you can feel the muscles squeezing them, it's astonishing. It's like nothing you ever imagined.

The two of you stay together all night. She goes down on you, properly dammed, and you discover that with a little lube on the other side of the rubber, it can feel amazingly good. You come over and over again. And once you come, once she does, it isn't over. She doesn't need half an hour to get her libido back. No, she keeps on going—even when she's exhausted, she can still move a finger slowly, rub a thigh between your legs, up against your naked cunt. She likes to talk dirty, too: she whispers words in languages you don't know into your ear as she fucks you. She tells you that she's half Filipino, one quarter Chicana, one eighth Indian, one eighth Greek. It's a gorgeous mix; you've never seen anyone who looks like her, who talks like her. Who moves like her. She says she wants to take you home and fuck you properly. She says she wants to pull out her harness and dildo and fuck your cunt, your ass. She promises you all sorts of things and then tells you that she doesn't always keep her promises. She teases you, bringing you up to a peak, over and over, making you wait until she's ready, until she's up there with you and you can tumble down over the other side together.

Finally, people start leaving. Carol's wandering around, saying good-byes. Robert's cleaning up. You and Rose have finally stopped, too, but you're both utterly exhausted, you can't possibly move. You're draped over each other, a tangle of arms and legs and breasts, entirely naked aside from the gold cross hanging around Rose's neck. Carol comes up to you then, sits down cross-legged beside you, cheerfully naked, too.

"Hey, Rose. You didn't tell me that the girl you were bringing was your girlfriend."

You open your mouth to protest, to say that you're not actually Rose's girlfriend, that she doesn't date roommates, that this was just one night, one incredible night. But before you can say anything, Rose is laying a lazy, soft finger across your lips and saying to Carol, "So I don't tell you everything. It's good for you to be surprised once in a while."

Carol grins. "Well, you two certainly have some great energy—you were a real inspiration to the rest of the room. Keep it up. But now get out of my house, so I can go to bed!"

Somehow you get up, get dressed, and walk out the door, still a little stunned. Girlfriend? Did Rose just imply that she wants you to be her girlfriend?

Once you're safely out the door and into the early morning fog, you turn to Rose, not at all sure what to say. You signed up for a night of woman-on-woman sex—it was amazing, but you don't know if you're ready to turn into a full-time lesbian. Before you can say that, before you can say anything, she leans forward and kisses you again. You can't resist that, and you kiss her back for an endless time. When you finally disengage, a little dizzy, she again manages to speak before you do.

"Didn't mean to jump the gun there, chica. But I'd be up for it if you want to try this again sometime. After sleeping some and eating some, 'cause I'm about ready to drop dead right now. And church, of course—it's Sunday." Rose smiles at you, her eyes sparkling.

Church? You didn't even know Rose was religious. There's so much you don't know about her. You want to learn more, though. "But what about the whole no-roommates rule?"

"Well, you could always move out. . . ." She laughs at your startled face, then starts both of you walking down the street, back toward the bus stop. It's going to be a long ride back to the apartment. "Kidding, kidding. No, but seriously, I think I'm ready to toss the whole no-roommates rule. It's a dumb rule." She takes your hand, squeezes it in hers. "So, what do you say? Dinner tonight?"

What the hell—it doesn't commit you to turning lesbian or anything, and it sure sounds like fun. You like Rose, you like this city, you really love all the orgasms. You're having an terrific time, and you're eager to see what happens next.

"Sure. Sounds good." And you walk down the street, two women holding hands, a bit unsteady on their heels but happy.

THE END

I'd want to travel." You pull back a little, not letting go but enough that you can look up into John's eyes. You need to see his reactions.

"Sure, of course. Anywhere you want to go." He's talking fast, almost babbling. It's charming. "The business is going great, like I said. I can take some time off; I've got plenty of money in the bank. . . ."

What else would you need? "And I want to work. Not just stay home and have babies." You've enjoyed working, depositing that nice fat paycheck. You couldn't earn as much in Indiana, but you know you could bring home something worthwhile.

"That's fine—heck, more money can't be bad, right?" He looks worried, the lines on his forehead deepening. "But Katie, you want to have a kid or two? Eventually?"

You didn't mean to scare him. "Yes, I think I do. Just not right away. And I don't want to stop working when I have them, which means you'll have to help at home."

He smiles. "I can do that. I used to change my little brother's diapers."

"I didn't know that." You can't really imagine it: football John, changing diapers!

John kisses your forehead gently. "There's a lot you don't know about me, Katie. I'm not the guy you thought I was."

"Maybe you aren't." You look up at him and then step back into his arms, burying your face against his shoulder. You're not sure you can look at him while you say the next part. But you need to say it, need to know how he'll react. You're not demure Indiana-Katie anymore. "And I want to have lots of sex. In different positions. And oral sex. Maybe with sex toys. I might even want to tie you up."

John stiffens for a moment, then he takes a deep breath and relaxes again. In fact, he seems more than relaxed—he seems a little turned on. Is that his cock getting hard against you?

"Sure, Katie. I'm sorry I was such a stick in the mud before. I had some weird ideas about the kinds of things you didn't do with the girl you were going to marry. I got over them pretty quick once you left. I couldn't stop thinking about all the things I wished I'd done with you."

You say the next words softly; you're not sure how he'll take them. "Johnny, I don't want to get married. Not yet, and maybe not ever. Let's just date for a while and see how it goes, OK? I'm not the same girl I was when I left Indiana; you might not like the new me."

He's gone very still as you talk. He hesitates before asking, "Does that mean you're coming back with me?"

"If you're sure you want me to." You're not sure when exactly you decided to go; somewhere in that list of questions, maybe. Or maybe before that, in the first moment when you saw him in your hallway, when his simple presence stopped your breath. When you love someone for years, the way you loved John, it's always there inside you afterward, lurking, waiting to ambush you. If he hadn't changed, you never would have considered going back. But now here he is, different and new. Full of possibilities. And looking like home nonetheless.

"Yes. Absolutely, positively sure." He's pulled back again, and he's grinning wide enough that you can count all his teeth.

"Then I guess I am." And he's kissing you then, kissing you like he plans to kiss you all the way back to Indiana. The kiss heats you up, hardens your nipples and makes your pussy pulse. His cock is definitely hard now, and you can feel every inch of heat where his body presses against yours. John's hands curl in your hair; your hands are on his back, pulling him closer. The buzzer rings, and you ignore it. Out of the corner of your eye, you can see all your roommates peeking out of their rooms—they'll handle Stripperguy. Right now all you care about is kissing John—and in a little while, pulling him back into your bedroom to show him some of what you've learned in San Francisco. It'll be wonderful to go home, but nothing says you have to leave right away. . . .

THE END

This is definitely weird, but exciting, too. You smile at him, and he takes that as invitation enough to sit down facing you, also cross-legged. You try not to stare at that huge cock, but he catches you sneaking peeks at it, and he smiles. "May I kiss you?"

"Yes . . ." You don't even know his name, and that's part of what's exciting. He bends forward and puts his hands behind your neck, pulling you into a deep kiss. His mouth is open, his tongue pressing insistently against your lips until they open, too, pushing inside and opening you up, flooding you with heat. He pulls away long enough to ask, "Lie down with me?" and you say yes—you want to know what it'll be like, kissing him with your bodies pressed together. And then you're lying down, and his mouth is on yours again, kissing you fiercely. His hands are busy unbuttoning your shirt, pulling it off. Is he supposed to ask your permission? You're not sure, and it doesn't seem to matter—you want your shirt off, you want his skin against yours. His hands move down to your breasts, squeeze them hard—nothing about this man is gentle, but you don't care. He's pinching the nipples through your bra, then, impatiently, pulling down the cups, baring your breasts. You reach to unhook the bra, sliding it off while his mouth moves to your nipples, sucking and biting them, and his hands move to your ass, pulling it close, squeezing and kneading your ass cheeks roughly. His body is between your legs, then sliding up, up so that his cock is thrusting hard against the thin fabric of your panties, and you don't know how this has happened so hard, so fast—you're dizzy with it, but it all feels so good. And you're reaching to peel off your panties, because right now you want nothing more than for him to fuck you, when he reaches out and grabs your wrist, squeezing so hard that you let out a yelp of pain.

"Not here. I want to be naked when I fuck you—really naked. I want to put my naked cock into your naked cunt. But there's no way we'd get away with that here. Let's ditch this joint and go someplace where we can really party."

Really naked. You suddenly get what he's saying. This is a safe-sex party, and this guy isn't into safe sex. You're on the pill—John had insisted on it, just in case, even though you always used condoms, too—you won't get pregnant. You know you ought to be worrying about diseases, but it's tough to think about it when his mouth has descended on yours again, devouring you, when his hips are grinding against yours, his incredible cock sliding in and out between your thighs, against your soaked panties, driving you crazy, up the fucking wall. It's hard to think.

• *If you say no*, PLEASE TURN TO PAGE 211.

• *If you say yes*, PLEASE TURN TO PAGE 33.

None of you really sleep that night. One or the other dozes off here and there, but mostly you stay awake, talking, touching. You watch Jamie go down on Michael; Jamie watches Michael go down on you. Somehow you'd thought that there'd be more of everyone fucking at once, but instead, it's mostly pairing off, then changing pairs. It's easier to manage the bodies that way. There's lots of cuddling, too. And talking—at some point during the night, you tell the boys about John. They agree that he wasn't worth sticking around Indiana for. Jamie talks about a few of his previous lovers, but they were clearly long ago and far away. Michael doesn't bother talking about anyone else. He tells you about being a boy in San Francisco—what it was like to grow up as a boy, big and strong and liking boys.

Before dawn, the two of them manage to doze off at the same time, curled around you. You lie there, your head resting on Michael's chest, Jamie's head against your breast. What a strange place you've come to. It was an incredible night, but you can already see that there might be problems in the future. There were moments, during the night, when you were jealous of Michael—and of Jamie. Times when you didn't want to share, when you didn't want Jamie to turn away from kissing you to kiss Michael. But there were more times when you smiled to see them touch, when it made you happy to see how happy they made each other. And when both of them were focusing all their attention on you— whew! You're utterly exhausted now. They'd both fucked you, Jamie more than once. And you'd lost track of all the other orgasms they'd given you. At one point it had almost seemed like a contest, to see which of them could make you come harder, faster, more often. An excellent use for male competitive urges, in your opinion. Clearly, if you're willing to deal with the potential emotional risks, you could have a hell of a lot of fun here.

And maybe something more. Michael does have some interesting emotions under all that glorious preening and pride. He can be incredibly sweet. And when Jamie looks at you with his eyes all wide and vulnerable—well, it feels like your heart's about to stop right then. You want to reach out and take him into your arms and hold him for a very long time.

You're not in love or anything, not yet, but the potential's there. You can see it when you look at them both. You can feel it. It's not what you expected when you left Indiana—even knowing San Francisco's reputation, you didn't expect to end up in a threesome with two gorgeous men. But if you're all very careful, if you're honest with one another, and especially if you keep striking the kind of sparks you've been striking, you might build something amazing.

You almost want to wake them up again, tell them what you've been thinking, feeling. But they look so tired. Instead, you close your eyes, try to catch a little sleep in the arms of your men. Outside your window, the sun is rising.

THE END

"No . . ." You can barely get the word out, but you manage it. You may be crazy horny right now, but you're not stupid. If you did what he wanted, you could get some embarrassing disease—or a more serious one. You'd be risking your life, and no sex, no matter how good it might be, would be worth that. You can't quite believe he'd even ask you for it. You say it again, more firmly, more loudly. "No!" Loud enough that a few people turn their heads, checking up on you. He stops moving, pulls away.

"Your choice, lady. Have fun." And he gets up, walking away, leaving you shaking. What the hell was that about?

You sit up, wrap your arms around your knees. It takes a while before you calm down. By the time you do, the puppy pile in the corner has grown as more and more of the party has joined in. The aggressive guy has gone; presumably he found someone more willing to party than you were. There are a few couples here and there, but you can't spot any more single guys. You can go over and join the pile; maybe you'll have some fun there. It looks friendly, at any rate. But part of you is totally weirded out.

It's not like none of the guys in Indiana ever would have pushed for sex without condoms; you heard plenty of stories from your girlfriends. But you never experienced that kind of pressure yourself. Do you really want to be here, experiencing new and difficult things every day, trying to live in this strange city? You're still shaking, sitting there in just your panties, with your pussy wet and your mouth sore from his rough kisses. Do you want to join the pile in the corner, see if you can still have some fun here, at this party, in this city? Or do you want to just give up? You could be home in half an hour; you could be packed and on a bus by morning. It might be dull in Indiana, but it would be safe.

Of course, you could also try calling Peter. Maybe you didn't give him enough of a shot—maybe he'd still be willing to go out with you. He did seem really sweet, and while he was sexy, he wasn't pushy about it. Peter's a definite possibility.

- *If you want to call Peter and see if he's still interested,* PLEASE TURN TO PAGE 173.

- *If you're tired of dealing with this city and want to go back to Indiana,* PLEASE TURN TO PAGE 112.

- *If you're willing to brave the pile of bodies,* PLEASE TURN TO PAGE 214.

"Sorry, not interested." You aren't so used to turning people down, but Rose had been very clear about the rules. If you want to say no, say no. And be clear about it. "Your loss." And he's gone, walking away.

You sit there a minute longer, considering. You could just wander around, but the group in the corner looks really interesting. You could pick up a single guy anywhere—only at a sex party could you try something like that! The more you watch them, the more turned on you get. They're all naked—if you were going to join them, maybe you should be naked, too? You unbutton your shirt and slide it off. Trying not to think about whether anyone is watching you undress, you undo your bra and remove it. You don't feel quite up to taking off the panties, though—maybe someone in the pile will do it for you. You stand up.

→

Y ou take a deep breath and walk across the room, conscious of all the eyes on you. It helps that everyone else is pretty much naked by now, including both of your hosts. In your panties, you might be the most dressed person in the room. You reach the pile but aren't quite sure how to join in. You sit down on the floor, cross-legged again. At least now you're on their level. In front of you, three people are busy licking the body of a fourth, a rather hairy man. He's not particularly attractive, but he's not unattractive either, and he smells faintly of vanilla. It's nice. One of the three looks up, catches your eye, and smiles. "Want to join us?"

"If it's OK with you?" you ask the hairy man. He opens his blissfully closed eyes long enough to look at you, smile, and nod. Then he closes his eyes again, moaning as one of the three starts licking a nipple. You bend down, hesitantly, and take the other nipple in your mouth. It tastes good, faintly salty with sweat. You suck gently and are rewarded with another moan of pleasure. This is kind of fun.

You move down, kissing a path down his stomach. You shift so you're kneeling; it's easier to reach the interesting places. His cock is already sheathed in rubber, and you hesitate only a moment before taking it in your mouth. It tastes, well, rubbery. But the shape of it feels good, filling your mouth. You slide down, taking it as far as you can—which is pretty damn far, as it turns out. It's thick, but not that long. Your lips go all the way down to the base of the condom, and your mouth and tongue move gently, sucking and licking. It turns you on; you can feel yourself getting wet again, your thighs slightly slick against each other. That's when you feel a hand against your hip. You freeze for a second, glance back. A slender Asian man is sitting beside you, his hand now hovering just above your panties. "May I?" he asks quietly. You're not sure exactly what he's asking, but he's kind of cute. Shit—why the hell not? You nod a yes, as best you can with a thick cock in your mouth. He pulls your panties down to your knees, and you lift up long enough for him to pull them off entirely. Now you're just as naked as the rest of them.

You keep sucking as he moves behind you, and then he's pressing a wet dam against your ass, a startling coolness. You can't quite tell what he's doing, but it feels good—it feels really good. You think he's using his tongue to press the dam against your asshole, drawing little circles that make your thighs shiver. Then he's sliding two fingers into your cunt, rubbing another against your clit, and someone has started sucking one of your breasts; you have no idea who, but you don't care anymore. Your eyes are closed; you're just moving up and down on that cock, still licking and sucking but not thinking about it anymore. You're focused on the sweet tingle in your nipple, the shivery wetness moving around your asshole, the incredible pleasure of cunt and ass, of fingers moving at exactly the right tempo, plunging in and out, bringing you higher and higher until finally you come, moaning around the cock in your throat. And then they start over.

→

You can't keep track of time, or of bodies. You touch a man, gently, your fingers tracing the shape of his arms, his legs. You caress his balls, then his hard, long cock. You're wet, dripping. You slide a condom on, then climb atop his cock. While you ride it, his hands are busy on your breasts; someone else is kissing you, and someone else is kissing him. He rolls you over and begins to fuck you hard as someone pulls your wrists up above your head. Someone's mouth is busy on your throat, your breasts—no, two people are licking your breasts, sucking your nipples, and another is kissing you, and he's still fucking you, he's inexhaustible, and you're coming and coming and coming again, and then he's inside you again, or maybe it's not him, maybe it's someone else instead. You're losing track, losing yourself in the sweaty limbs, the slick of skin against skin, the blur of wet mouths moving on you, on your mouth, your breasts, your cunt.

Somewhere in there are condoms, dental dams, rubber gloves, but you can't even tell, not with a lubed finger sliding into your ass, a mouth gentle then hard on your clit, two, three fingers in your cunt, slipping up, up inside you, curling against that spot that makes you moan, makes you scream, makes you flood until the sheets spread over the floor are soaked, and still you're coming and coming, losing yourself in the joyous movement of bodies arching against one another, until you collapse exhausted, gasp deep breaths, still your heart—and then it all happens again.

This is why you came to this city: this intense pleasure, this endless satisfaction. You can't imagine anything better.

• PLEASE RETURN TO THE TOP OF THE PAGE; IT'S AN ENDLESS ORGY.

S hit, it's cold here in the mornings. Jacket. Got to remember the jacket. You walk quickly down the street to the corner, turn, and push open the door of the café. Three Asian students are sitting on some couches, a stack of medical textbooks in front of them, along with huge cups of coffee. A smiling brown-skinned woman stands behind the counter—in the single day you've been in this city, you've seen more ethnic people than you'd see in a month in Indiana. It's nice.

Two black guys are sitting at a table, playing chess. One of them looks up and catches your eye. It's the guy from the stairwell, Rose's ex. What the heck was his name? He smiles, a slow grin that wanders across his face. His eyes slide down, from your face to your neck to the thin sweater that clings to your chest. You cross your arms in front of you—you just know your nipples are sticking out from the cold, and in that sweater . . . He smiles more broadly but turns his eyes politely back to the game.

Your mom told you not to talk to strangers. Really cute strangers who smile at your breasts are definitely off-limits. Does this guy count as a stranger? You turn and walk to the counter and order coffee. But by the time it arrives, a few more people have come in and sat down, filling up the remaining tables. The only seat left is with the two chess players. You take a quick gulp of your coffee, then walk over. "Mind if I sit down?"

The older man just shakes his head, eyes still fixed on the chessboard. But the other, the ex, looks up and smiles again.

"Hi, Kathryn. Good to see you again." He must read the confusion on your face, because he grins a little wider. "I'm Peter. Have you forgotten me already? I'm crushed." He holds his hand out for you to shake. You take his hand in yours, blushing. He has his shirtsleeves rolled up; his hands are attached to slender wrists and smooth, dark forearms. The rest is covered by the shirt, but your mind insists on filling in the blanks—lean, muscled upper arms and sleek shoulders, like a swimmer. That's his build—long and lean. Elegant. What would it be like, your body against his, naked, your breasts against his smooth chest? Somehow, you're sure it's smooth. Your nipples are so hard that they ache a little, and your legs are getting wobbly. You have to stop thinking like this! Just because a man smiles at you is no reason to imagine having sex with him. But still—you wish you'd waited and taken that shower before coming out.

You pull up a chair and sit, balancing your coffee precariously on the edge of the table. Peter moves the chessboard over to make more room, eliciting a muttered grumble from his friend.

"That's Jake—don't mind him. He's always like that when he's lost a game and isn't ready to admit it. So, you settling in OK? Getting along with Rose and the boys?" He seems really interested, his dark eyes fixed on yours. You don't think he's flirting, but he does seem to care about your answer.

→

They're really nice." You could stop there, but Peter seems friendly, inviting. He makes you want to tell him more—and you'd like to talk to someone about all this. "Though I have to admit, it was a bit of a shock. Sally didn't tell me that two of my roommates would be gay, or that the other one works as a stripper." You try to laugh a little, pass it off as a funny joke. You're not sure how funny it is.

Peter grins sympathetically. "It takes some getting used to. To be honest, I never really liked Rose's job. It was a weird thing, having a girlfriend who's a stripper."

"Is that how you met her? At the club?" You don't want to think that of Peter; you hardly know him, but he doesn't seem the type of guy to visit strippers. Not that you know what kind of guy that is. Maybe they all go to see strippers, even the nice ones.

"No, no." He laughs softly. "I met her on campus—she's a grad student at Berkeley, in psych. I'm in math."

"She didn't say anything about school!" You hide your face in your coffee for a moment. Now you're feeling stupid—somehow you'd just assumed that stripping was all Rose did. She was so cute and bouncy; you couldn't imagine her as a grad student. Did she bounce in her classes, too?

"Rose is funny that way—she'd rather talk about stripping than about her classes. But really, she's pretty good at them; she's probably teaching one right now. The students love her."

"I bet. And you're a grad student too?"

"Post-doc, actually. I'm twenty-nine; older than I look."

Peter doesn't look more than twenty-four. He must be incredibly smart. He makes you feel dumb. Dumb and horny. Why didn't you at least brush your hair before leaving the apartment?

He's sliding his chair back. "Listen, I have a class soon, and I need to get back across the Bay. I can walk you to your door . . ."

"Sure—that'd be nice." That's more than just friendly, isn't it? Is Peter hitting on you? Do you want him to? What would you say if he did? You finish your coffee, leaving the cup on the table.

Peter gathers up some books and a notepad and slips them into a black bag. He slings the bag over his shoulder, nods to his friend, who nods back without looking up from the chessboard, and then courteously gestures for you to precede him. As you walk between crowded tables to the café door, you can feel him right behind you. He reaches out and pulls the door open; you slip through. You feel strangely aware of his body next to yours, the length of it walking beside you up the street.

You could turn and kiss the man walking next to you—you could take his hand and lead him to the park a few blocks away. You could find a secluded corner and peel off your clothes in the sunshine. You could unbutton that crisp white shirt; you could slide your hands down to his pants, undoing the top button, unzipping them slowly. You could push his naked body down to the grass and stroke his cock until it stood up straight and firm. You could straddle him, your already wet pink pussy sliding easily down over his thick dark cock. You could bring his hands up to your breasts, where he would gently knead them, pinching the nipples as you arch back, moving slowly up and down, up and down in the bright sunlight . . .

"So, here you are."

You've reached the apartment gate, a massive metal wall with an intercom. Peter smiles down at you. Your face feels hot. Are you blushing? Can he tell what you were just thinking? He's only an inch or two away; you could reach out and touch him. You could ask him to dinner sometime—you might end up in bed, if not actually in the park. In Indiana, you'd have waited for the guy to ask you.

"I'll see you around?" There, you said it. It wasn't quite asking him out, but it was something. Sally would be proud.

"Sure." Peter's smile broadens. His teeth are very white. "I'm at the café with Jake most mornings; we're both chess fiends. Stop by and look me up. I'd like that."

He'd like that! You want to look him up and down and up some more. And not just look. "Is Jake a student, too?"

"Jake? No, Jake's a bum. Homeless. But a wicked chess player. Anyway, gotta run. I'll see you soon!" He grins, touches your arm lightly with one hand—a reassuring touch. Maybe a little more?

"See you soon."

And then he's gone, striding back to the bus stop.

You go upstairs and let yourself into an empty apartment—everyone else is out. It's nice, having the place to yourself. You have a long, decadent hot shower, then wrap yourself in a big fluffy towel and eat toast and Nutella in the sunny kitchen. San Francisco is feeling a lot friendlier than it did last night. Maybe it's the sunshine—maybe it's the cute guy who was flirting with you. You think. Maybe. You climb back into bed and doze for a while; Rose had woken you up way too early. But before long, it's time to get up, get dressed in jeans and T-shirt. Suddenly, Rose is there at your bedroom door, fully dressed for once, bouncing again.

"Hey, chica! It's gorgeously sunny out—you're going to see the city at its best! So, what sounds appealing? Corsets and leather? Vintage style on the cheap? Or should we just get some sexy lingerie?"

Corsets and leather sound intriguing, the sort of thing a sexy romance heroine might wear, but you're sure they're way out of your price range, and probably out of your league. You'd just feel silly. Vintage stuff would be great for wandering around, but the Lusty Lady audition is tonight, and sometime in the night, you decided that you at least want to go take a look around the club, see what you think of it.

"I know! Let's go to the mall! I love Victoria's Secret—they have huge dressing rooms, big enough for two, so I can really take a good look and let you know what works for you, and you can do the same for me. I've been meaning to get some new thongs. This is going to be fun!"

• PLEASE TURN TO PAGE 44.

Why should you have to ask him out? Isn't that the guy's job? John had asked you out, way back in high school, and so has every other guy who hit on you since then. That's the way it's supposed to be—or maybe you're just too chicken. But if you're chicken, then that's the way you are. You're going to have to live with it. And there must be guys in San Francisco who aren't as lacking in initiative as Peter is. You'll have to keep looking.

You say a polite good night to Peter, closing the door behind him. He doesn't make any attempt to ask you out—the big wimp. You say good night to your roommates and go to bed, hoping tomorrow will bring a more aggressive, exciting man into your life.

➤

Saturday you wake up early and eager—you're going to your first sex party tonight! You're a bit nervous, too, but you're trying not to think about that. You spend a while in front of the mirror, looking at your body from different angles. It looks OK, but you wish you'd done some more sit-ups in the last few days. You spend an hour doing various exercises in your room; it won't make any immediate difference, but it makes you feel better about the idea of getting naked in front of strangers tonight.

You wander out to find your roommates having breakfast. Jamie and Michael are arguing amiably about the relative virtues of French toast versus pancakes; Rose has solved the problem by piling some of both on her plate. You join in, adding some sliced strawberries and maple syrup. It's awfully nice living with roommates who can cook—it's almost as good as having your mom cooking for you.

You spend most of the afternoon just hanging around. There's some group cleanup of the apartment, some grocery shopping, some discussion of chores and the splitting of utility bills. There's also a lot of chatting, silliness, laughter. These are good people—smart, funny, nice. The hours fly by, and before you know it, it's time to go. You're getting ready with Rose, and the guys are offering comments, suggestions, a few lewd remarks. You try on a dozen different outfits before you settle on something you're happy with, something that makes you feel sexy. Rose lets you have just one glass of wine before you go—apparently Carol has strict rules about no drunks at her sex parties. Still, the one glass does help you relax—and then it's time to go.

• PLEASE TURN TO PAGE 70.

Y ou come back to the apartment to find Michael waiting there. Jamie had called him from the office and given him the green light, so he'd taken a late lunch and come home to see you. You manage to squeeze in a quickie before you have to shower and rush off to your job interview. You arrive a little late, convinced that you've blown it, but they give you the job anyway: a three-month contract to write from home. Good deal.

Peter comes by for dinner, and you feel a brief pang of regret, looking at that lean, dark body. But you aren't about to try adding Peter into the mix. And besides, talking to Rose makes it clear that Peter is a traditional sort of guy who would definitely not be up for sharing you with Michael. And Michael is too much fun to give up.

Saturday you go antiquing with Jamie and have a really good time. He knows a remarkable amount about old furniture, and he has a quiet, dry humor that catches you by surprise more than once. You have so much fun that you agree to go antiquing with him every Saturday.

As for the sex with Michael—it's intoxicating. You're mostly trying to not have sex when Jamie's home, which isn't so hard to manage, since Michael can pretty much set his own schedule at work. He goes in when he wants, so you have plenty of long, leisurely mornings of lying naked in that vast bed, Michael's massive body pressed against you, his hands roaming eagerly over every inch of your skin. Plenty of kisses, on lips and neck and breasts and thighs. He loves going down on you—he's willing to do it for what seems like hours, coming up damp and musky to kiss your lips and let you breathe, then going right back down again. He's teaching you more new positions than you knew existed: your current favorite is up against the wall, his strong body holding you up easily, your legs wrapped around his waist and his cock pounding into you. But next week might be a different one.

There are some tense moments. Rose is full of doom and gloom, predicting that this is all going to end badly, but she has a thing about roommates dating. There are definitely moments when you feel jealous—when you see Michael ruffle Jamie's hair, walking down the hall, or even when Jamie just says, "Sweetheart, can you pick up some coffee from the market?" Little things ambush you. And while you fall asleep easily most nights, there are a few when you lie awake, trying to hear if there are any noises coming from their bedroom, wishing Michael were here with you, instead of there with Jamie.

The worst comes on a weekend. Jamie had Michael last night; you're going to spend tonight, Friday night, with him. You want to do something romantic; you buy theater tickets, make reservations at a nice Italian restaurant downtown. You've gotten your first full paycheck, so you feel like you can splurge. You take a long shower, play with the showerhead a bit, get all worked up. You don't even let yourself come, because you want to be nice and aroused for Michael; you figure maybe you can get a quickie in with him before you head out to dinner. You get yourself all dolled up, all excited, and when Michael comes home, you meet him with a kiss at the door. That's when he says:

"Kathryn, I'm so sorry. Jamie just called—he's miserably sick. I'm going to go get him from the office, bring him home. And then I think we ought to stay in; I just can't go out and have fun when he's feeling terrible. Is that OK?"

→

There isn't really anything you could say to that, is there? You say it's OK, of course, and you try to be gracious, and Jamie does look awful when he gets home, so it isn't like he's having any great fun with Michael sitting by his bedside, holding his hand. You don't have any right to get angry, but you are angry, you're pissed off. It isn't fair that you have to share Michael with someone else, that your plans got canceled and you can't do a damn thing about it. You want Michael to be holding your hand in a nice dark theater—holding your hand, and then touching you all over with his hands afterward.

You spend a good week being mad at both of them, feeling angry and upset and helpless and lost. You come really close to calling the whole thing off so you can go look for a guy of your own, all your own. Finally you talk to them about it—an all-night conversation that leaves all three of you exhausted. You end up reassured that they both care about you, they're both committed to making this work, to taking your emotions and needs seriously. You can deal with the jealousy, the insecurity, but dealing with those feelings isn't any fun at all.

Mostly, those feelings don't last, though.

What does seem to last is the pleasure of it all, the intensity, the incredible way Michael makes you feel. The attention he pays to you, to your body. The growing fondness you have for Jamie. The way they both try to check in with you, see how you're feeling, make sure you're OK. The laughter at the breakfast table, despite Rose glowering in the background. The occasional three-way hugs, when Michael grabs both of you and pulls you close, beaming. The funny, wry grin that Jamie gives you then, and the delicious sense of sharing a secret, a knowledge of Michael, an appreciation for his goofy and endearing ways.

It's an incredible gift Jamie's given you, and you're determined to take good care of it. You're not sure where this will end up—maybe you and Michael will fall in love. Sometimes you think you already love him. You might even love them both, despite not being attracted to Jamie. Maybe you'll get your own apartment nearby someday, maybe you'll date someone else, too. Maybe it won't work out long-term, maybe you'll get too jealous, or Jamie will. Maybe there'll be tears and explosions.

But that's the danger of love, isn't it? You can be as careful as you want, but in the end, love rises up and overwhelms you. All this relationship complexity has forced you to think about love in a way you never took the time to before. You have long conversations with Jamie about it while antiquing, coming up with goofy metaphors that are oddly satisfying.

Recently you decided that love is like sailing a small boat on a very wide ocean; all you can do is carefully trim the sails and try not to fall overboard when the storms come up. Sometimes you swallow a mouthful of salt water. Sometimes you're rising high on the crest of an impossible wave. However it ends up, it's an incredible ride, and you wouldn't have wanted to miss it.

THE END

You pull back a little, turn away, busy yourself with trying on another bra. If Rose is flirting with you, clearly the polite thing to do is ignore it. Try on clothes. Make pleasant conversation.

"So . . . anything exciting happening this weekend ?" Oh, that sounds so lame—but it's better than "Were you just flirting with me?" Much better. Much safer.

Rose hesitates. "Actually, there's a party at Carol Queen's Saturday night . . . if you'd like to go, I can get you in."

"It's hard to get into?" You'd heard about exclusive private parties, but you'd never known anyone famous enough to have them in Indiana. It sounds like it could be a lot of fun.

"Well, she's pretty exclusive about the guest list for her parties. They're sex parties. Mixed gender—men with men, women with women, men with women. Group sex. That kind of thing." Rose is looking sideways at you, curious to see how you'll react.

Group sex? Is this what you want? Won't that mean more awkward overtures from women, or maybe from unattractive men? This is all too much. You came to San Francisco for adventure, but more finding-a-nice-sexy-guy adventure. Not group sex, or women, or strip clubs, for that matter. Have you been giving off the wrong signals? Is that why Rose thought you might be interested in this kind of weirdness? Is that why Michael kissed you, despite being gay and having a boyfriend? Maybe you've given them the wrong impression. You need to make it clear that you aren't into that kind of thing. Not even a little bit. All you really want is a guy of your own.

"I'm not really a sex-party kind of girl, Rose. And actually, I don't think strip clubs are my thing, either." You don't want to offend her, but you really don't want her to get the wrong idea about you. "The shopping was fun, but I think I'd better pass on the rest of it."

Rose shrugs. "Up to you, chica. I'll see you back at the apartment, then." She pulls on her clothes and slips out the door, leaving you with a handful of lingerie and a slight feeling of disappointment. Maybe you wanted her to try to talk you into it? Too late now. . . .

→

The next few days are awkward. You don't feel comfortable around your roommates; you find yourself avoiding them. Taking long walks in the city. Burying yourself in work. You get the tech-writing job, which is great, because it makes a perfect excuse to hide from them. You need to reestablish yourself in their eyes. You're not a sex-crazed maniac; you're just a nice, normal girl who works hard and wouldn't mind meeting a nice, normal guy some day. You even skip the Friday-night roommate dinner; it's all too much for you. You spend the evening working at the library instead.

You spend Saturday being a tourist, visiting Chinatown and North Beach. You drink an Irish whiskey alone at a café surrounded by a busy crowd. San Francisco is full of interesting characters, but you don't know them. You wish you had somebody to talk to. You pay for your drink and head out into the chilly evening. The light is changing over Coit Tower. You catch a bus back toward the apartment. As you get off the bus, you realize you're not quite ready to face Rose or Michael. You could walk around the neighborhood while it gets dark. But as you pass the café on the corner, you can't help glancing at the crowd of people inside and are startled to see a face you recognize. It's the same guy, Peter. He did say he came to the coffee shop often. He looks intent on another chess game with Jake, but maybe he wouldn't mind if you just went in and said hi. It would be nice to hear a friendly voice.

You squeeze past the sofas crowded with sprawling people. Peter looks up, smiles when he sees you, and pulls over an extra chair. You sit down beside him; your legs are almost touching. Not quite.

"Hey, we missed you at dinner last night."

"You were there?" Right, right—they had said that he often came. You could have spent hours talking to Peter if you'd only remembered. But at least he looks happy enough to see you now. "Sorry I missed it. I was pretty busy working."

"Working?"

You fill him in, telling him about the project. It's interesting, actually. You're creating a user manual for genealogy software. As it turns out, he's something of an amateur genealogy buff; he knows the names of all of his great-great-great-grandparents and when every single one of them came to America. You're impressed. You both get engrossed in the conversation to the point that Jake snorts, gets up, and leaves the table and the half-finished chess game without a word. You blush but keep talking to Peter.

Eventually the café closes, but you don't want to stop talking. You walk down the street past an Ethiopian restaurant that he loves. You've never had Ethiopian food. He says it's like pancakes and stew, really. That sounds kind of strange but not too awful.

"I'd be willing to try it," you say. "I guess," looking at him slyly and wondering why you made it sound so suggestive.

It's only when you've wandered back to your apartment and stopped in front that Peter finally kisses you, his long body bending down so his lips can touch yours. It's a sweet, sweet kiss, and you lean into it, your mouth opening under his. Your hands come up, press against his chest. It's firm under his shirt, muscled. You wish you could feel his bare skin. His kiss rushes through you, sending tingles to the tips of your fingers, your toes. Your tongue darts out, touches his. You moan softly under your breath. His hands come up, brush through your hair. You could stand here kissing him for hours . . . but he breaks away.

"I'm sorry, Kathryn. I didn't mean to kiss you like that, without asking. I don't know what happened."

"Did you hear me complaining?" You can't stop smiling at him. He smiles for a minute, too, then turns solemn again.

"Still—I don't want to rush things. I'd like to take you on a real date. If that's OK. Can I call you tomorrow?"

"I'd like that. You know the number."

He nods, then bends down, presses one more quick kiss on your lips. "Good night, Kathryn. Sleep well."

And then he's walking away, down the street, leaving you to unlock your door and climb the steps, still feeling that last kiss on your lips.

• PLEASE TURN TO PAGE 175.

Y ou walk out into the kitchen, pour yourself a cup of coffee, say good morning. They say good morning back, in chorus. How cute. You've decided to talk to Jamie, but how do you get him to talk to you? Maybe you just ask?

"Um, Jamie?"

"Yes?" He's finishing his breakfast, standing up, rinsing his dishes.

"Are you free to talk sometime?"

He looks at you then—a sharp look but not unfriendly. "I think that'd be a good idea, actually. Are you free for lunch?"

"Lunch?" Today? That's only a few hours away. "Sure, lunch would be fine."

"Great. Michael can tell you how to get to my office. I'm looking forward to it. Gotta run now." He puts the dishes in the rack, drying his hands, drops a kiss on Michael's forehead, and walks down the hall.

You plop down in the third chair, a little stunned. That went very fast.

Michael pats your hand consolingly. "It'll be fine, Katie. Now, about that job interview . . ."

The next few hours pass much too quickly.

• PLEASE TURN TO PAGE 39.

He's not stopping. Michael's whispering across the table, whispering what he's going to do to you later, telling you how he's going to fuck you with your body up against the wall and his cock pounding into you. How he wants to fuck you all over the apartment—in the shower, on the floor, and especially on that old church pew. He's going to fuck you there, and then you're going to go down on him, you're going to kneel before him, sitting in that pew, and suck him hard, suck him dry. You can't help picturing that, kneeling there the way you used to kneel in church when you were a little girl, kneeling with Michael naked on the pew, like an fallen angel, his thighs spread apart, and his glorious cock thick and erect, waiting for your hungry mouth. Your whole body shivers; you're pulsing, contracting around his wet, moving hand.

And then he's pushing harder, faster. Your hand falls away from his cock—you can't pay attention to that now. His knees are hard against your thighs and his hand is sliding in and out, against your clit then back inside, and you're coming, coming hard enough that the world disappears, just explosions all through you, a lightning storm, a pleasure that's almost pain. Maybe you moan. Maybe you scream. You're not sure.

You open your eyes to the sound of clapping.

• PLEASE TURN TO PAGE 161.

This book was produced by Melcher Media, Inc.,
124 West 13th Street, New York, NY 10011.

Charles Melcher / Publisher
Duncan Bock / Editor in Chief
Carolyn Clark / Publishing Manager
Andrea Hirsh / Director of Production
Megan Worman / Assistant Editor

Book design by Elizabeth Van Itallie
Cover photograph by Howard Schatz, copyright © Schatz/Ornstein

Create Your Own Erotic Fantasy is based on an idea by Makoto Nakayama.

AUTHOR'S ACKNOWLEDGMENTS
David Horwich, for hosting me in Oakland while I, um, researched. Dan Percival,
for an essential introduction. Rachel Reynolds for the informative, if slightly
sticky, tour. The always impressive Carol Queen for invaluable advice, and for
hosting excellent parties—or so I'm told. Sherman Lewis and Owen Thomas,
for loaning me their old apartment in the fabulous Haight. Owen for his bike
shorts, too. Matthew Frank, for comments and criticism. And finally, Heather
Shaw, for notes on life in Indiana, though all errors and misrepresentations are
entirely my own. I have never lived in Indiana myself, so apologies to any
Hoosiers for maligning your fair state.

MELCHER MEDIA'S ACKNOWLEDGMENTS
John Meils, Lauren Marino, Allison Murray, Ritsuko Okumura, Lia Ronnen,
Mark Roy, Bill Shinker, and E. Beth Thomas.

MARY ANNE MOHANRAJ is the author of *Torn Shapes of Desire*, editor of *Aqua Erotica*
and *Wet: More Aqua Erotica*, and a consulting editor for *Herotica* 7. Her fiction has
appeared in many anthologies and publications, including *Herotica 6*, *Best American
Erotica 1999*, and *Best Women's Erotica 2000* and *2001*. Ms. Mohanraj lives in Chicago.